FIRE WINGS

Anthony Ryan

Illustrated by
KEVIN GOEKE

Dedicated to anyone who ever dreamed of flying.

AUTHOR'S NOTE

The following story takes place in the same world as my short story *The Hall of the Diamond Queen*. Although *Fire Wings* can be read in isolation, readers in search of the full back story to the tale of the Wraith Queen Sharrow-Met might wish to seek out *The Hall of the Diamond Queen* which can be found in the *Unbound* anthology published by Grim Oak Press. It's also available free to subscribers to my mailing list, find details of how to subscribe at anthonyryan.net.

With wings of fire did she burn away her sins
And with blood did she wash their stain from her soul.
the *Epic of Sharrow-Met*.

ONE

Exiles

THE SKULL STARED UP AT HIM WITH JUST ONE EMPTY eye socket, the other having been shattered, along with much of the surrounding bone, the natural consequence of colliding with bare rock after a prolonged fall. Angling his head, Shamil couldn't escape the sense that it was grinning at him, the oddly perfect half set of teeth gleaming as it caught the midday sun. He wondered if this unfortunate had actually laughed as they plummeted to their death, reflecting on the grim notion that, should the same fate befall him, he may also find some humour in it, or possibly just relief.

"I thought it might be a myth."

Shamil tensed at the sound of an unexpected voice, one hand instinctively reaching for his quiver whilst the other unslung the strongbow from his shoulder. The man who had spoken was perched on a flat-topped boulder a dozen yards away, wrapped in a plain grey cloak that matched the surrounding rock. Shamil blamed this for his failure to spot him sooner, and the fact that the wind was at his back, sweeping away any betraying scent of sweat. Such excuses, he knew, would have availed him little in the Doctrinate, and this particular failure likely to earn him at best a hard cuff to the head or at worst a full beating. But the Doctrinate was far away, and the fact that he was no longer bound by its strictures one of the few crumbs of comfort Shamil could cling to during his recent sojourn.

"The leap, I mean," the man in grey said, gesturing to the half-shattered skeleton as he climbed down from his perch. He took a long gulp from a leather flask as he approached, his gait and posture lacking a threat. As he neared, Shamil saw that he was perhaps twice his own age, stocky of frame, and sparse of hair, his broad features showing several days' worth of stubble. He bore no weapon, and his accoutrements consisted of just a leather satchel bulging with unseen contents and a small emerald pendant that hung around his neck on a copper chain.

The gem was small, but the slight glimmer of light within it provoked Shamil to step back and lower his bow, eyes averted in respect, something this unshaven grey-cloak seemed to find amusing.

"Your people still cling to the old servile ways, I see," he said, voice rich with mirth. He took another drink from his flask and Shamil's nostrils caught the sting of strong liquor. The man's eyes tracked over Shamil, taking in his hardy leather boots, the long-bladed dagger in his belt alongside his raptorile-tail whip, and the strongbow fashioned from ram's horn and ash. "What are you? Strivante? No, skin's too dark for that. Oskilna maybe?"

"Vilantre," Shamil said, still not daring to look at the stranger's face. "I bid you greeting, Master Mage …"

"Oh, don't." The mirth in the stocky man's voice slipped into weary disdain as he waved his flask dismissively. "Just … don't. Please." He waited for Shamil to raise his gaze before extending his hand. "Rignar Banlufsson, late of … well, too many places to mention but most recently the Crucible Kingdom. Yourself?"

"Shamil L'Estalt." He hesitated before grasping the proffered hand, finding it strong and the palm unexpectedly callused. This mage, it seemed, had not spent his days locked away in a tower poring over ancient texts. "Late of Anverest."

"The desert city?" Rignar's brow creased in surprise. "You've come a very long way, young man." His gaze grew sombre as it slipped from Shamil to the skull at his feet. "For an uncertain outcome, it must be said. Makes you wonder how far this one had to travel just to jump off a mountain."

"If he fell, it's because he was unworthy," Shamil stated, adding a note of forceful certainty to his voice. Like him, this man might be just another exile come in search of restored honour, but he thought it best to leave no doubt about his commitment to this course.

"She," Rignar corrected, taking another drink from his flask before nodding to the bones. "You can tell from the brows and the breadth of the pelvis. Clothes and hair all gone, so she's been here a good long while, whoever she was, she and all the others. There's a pile of bones on the other side of that ridge if you'd care to see."

"I wouldn't."

"As you wish." The mage shrugged and turned back to his boulder. "Come, you can sort out this fire. You strike me as a

lad with experience of the wilds, and although I've travelled far in my time, I've never really managed to learn the trick of starting a fire."

"You are newly arrived, then?" Shamil ventured, following the mage to a small pile of sticks within a circle of gathered stones.

"Barely an hour before you did." Rignar sighed as he resumed his seat on the boulder. "I had hoped some fellow exile would get here first, perhaps have even prepared a meal."

Shamil crouched at the fire's edge, keeping the surprise and suspicion from his face as he rearranged the twigs, his mind filled with dark conjecture on the magnitude of any crime that would see a mage forced to seek redemption as a sentinel.

"There's not enough kindling to catch a spark," he said. "And we'll need more wood if it's to burn for any length of time." He shifted, casting an uncertain glance at the crystal pendant around Rignar's neck. "Can't you … ?

"Certainly not," the mage sniffed, raising his nose in indignation that Shamil took a second to recognise as pretense, but not before he had begun to babble out an apology. "Best to conserve what power I still hold, lad," Rignar added with a faint grin, raising a pointed glance to the mountain looming above. "After all, who knows what awaits us tomorrow, eh?"

Shamil followed his gaze, eyes tracking over the slopes and cliffs forming the peak that had dominated his sight and his thoughts since it first came into view a week ago. It rose from the eastern extremity of the crescent-shaped mountain range known to those who dwelt in these lands as the Harstfelts, but to every other denizen of the Treaty Realms as Sharrow-Met's Shield.

The mountain they stood beneath was by far the tallest in the range, and considerably narrower. From a distance, it resembled a misshapen spearpoint fashioned by one of the more primitive desert tribes. Although born to a desert city, Shamil was no stranger to mountains. The Doctrinate would compel its students to endure months of hard living in the crags that formed the southern border with the raptorile dominion. Treacherous as those were, he had never scaled a peak so tall with flanks so sheer as those looming above.

"She named it well," he murmured, peering into the clouds misting the mountain's summit. "The Eyrie, for who but an eagle could call it home?"

"She didn't name it." Rignar's voice abruptly took on a dull, almost resentful note. Turning, Shamil found him staring at nothing, gaze unfocused as he drank from his flask with habitual automation. "Sharrow-Met," he added after a momentary silence. "She never named anything; that was all done by those who followed her after she ..."

His voice dwindled, and he spent a few more seconds staring before raising his flask to his lips, then grimacing upon finding it empty. "Oh well," he sighed, tossing the flask away with an air of finality. "The last wine to ever pass my lips. Wish I'd chosen a better vintage. They don't allow it up there, apparently." He clasped his hands together and got to his feet. "We should get to gathering wood. It would be best to greet our fellow despised with a warm camp, don't you think?"

• ✦ •

THE FIRE HAD GROWN TO A TALL CONE OF BRIGHT FLAME, and the sky shifted to a darker hue by the time more exiles arrived—a young woman about Shamil's own age and a tall, well-built man several years older. Although they shared the pale skin of the central and northern Treaty Realms, the mismatched attire and accents bespoke markedly different origins.

The young man wore his blond hair in thick braids, an iron band engraved with runes encircling his brow and a straight sword at his belt. A leather jerkin studded with flattened copper discs covered his torso, and he wore a bearskin cloak about his broad shoulders. As he introduced himself, he revealed a set of even white teeth in a smile, voice rich in both surety and humour. "Tolveg Clearwater of Wodewehl, good sirs. Well met we are, and friends we'll stay, I'm sure."

As he bowed, Shamil noted the scars on his neck. They were an extensive, overlapping matrix of injury that evidently proceeded down his back, also not long healed judging by their colour. Tolveg, however, didn't appear to feel any pain as he straightened, nodding in appreciation as Shamil and Rignar offered their own names in greeting.

The woman was a stark contrast to her companion, saying nothing as she crouched to extend her hands to the fire. Her hair was jet black, catching a silklike shine from the fire, and her skin even more pale than Tolveg's. It possessed a near alabaster whiteness that recalled the ancient marble statues of long-forgotten gods Shamil had seen during his journey north. Her cloak was of finely woven wool, and her soft leather trews and jerkin betrayed the hand of a skilled and no doubt expensive tailor. Her weapons consisted of two daggers, one on her belt and another smaller blade tucked into her boot. As she shuffled closer to the warmth, Shamil saw she also had a leather sling and pouch attached to the left side of her belt.

"This is Lyvia," Tolveg said, taking a seat beside Shamil on the fallen tree limb he and Rignar had harvested from the wooded slope below the ridge. "We met on the trail a few days ago." He raised an eyebrow at Shamil, his hearty tones subsiding into a sigh. "She doesn't say much."

Lyvia's eyes, as dark as her hair, flicked up at Tolveg, a small crease of irritation marring her smooth brow before she returned her full attention to the fire.

"You're from the Crucible Kingdom," Rignar said. His tone was that of a statement rather than a question, and Shamil saw a new depth of interest in the mage's face. He stared at the woman crouching by the fire with a strange, intense scrutiny that spoke of hard, perhaps unwelcome recognition.

"I am," she replied, voice quiet and flat in a clear signal that further conversation was not welcome.

"Ah, a Mara-Vielle accent—noble too." Rignar observed, undaunted. "Which house?" His voice held a depth of interest that failed to stir a response from Lyvia. Her lips remained firmly closed, and she kept her hands outstretched, refusing to turn.

"Gondarik, I'd say," Rignar said with a note of satisfactio. "So there's royal blood in your veins." He angled his head and leaned close. Shamil saw the woman tense, hands withdrawing to her belt. "*Her* blood. Not that I need a name to tell me that." His voice grew softer, eyes unblinking as he shifted to gain a better view of her face. "Just an inch or so taller and it would be as if she's risen to walk amongst us …"

"Put your eyes elsewhere, old man!"

Hearing her give full throat to her voice, Shamil found she possessed the oddest accent he had heard in all his travels. The words were spoken with a careful precision despite the rapidity with which she uttered them, the vowels soft and the consonants clearly enunciated. This, he realised, was the voice of ancient nobility. Royal blood indeed.

She rose to face Rignar, her face somehow managing to convey both a snarl and imperious disdain at the same time. "I'll not be gawped at! Mage or no. And my blood is not your concern."

Rignar reclined in the face of her anger, a half-smile playing over his lips as he raised his hands. "Spoken like a true queen," he said, which did little to calm Lyvia's ire.

"Well, I'm not a queen." She turned away from him, stalking to the opposite side of the fire to sit down, arms crossed and her back to them all. "I'm just a dishonoured, disgraced outcast, like each of you."

Silence reigned as her voice faded, although Tolveg apparently found such a thing intolerable. "I prefer 'honour-seeker', myself," he said. "For that is why we came here, is it not? And this is not my first journey to far-off lands, let me tell you. Once, I stood at my uncle's side when he captained a ship all the way through the ice shards to the lands of ash smoke where the gryphons still soar ..."

Shamil listened politely as the warrior continued his tale, finding much of it hard to credit, even though it was spoken with an earnest sincerity. The northman's tale wore on as Rignar unfurled a blanket to settle down to sleep, whilst Lyvia, plainly having already had her fill of Tolveg's voice, rose and walked off to seek shelter amongst the surrounding rocks. Eventually, once it became apparent this story was unlikely to have an end, Shamil abandoned courtesy and slumped down at the edge of the fire's glow. Wrapping his cloak around himself, he soon drifted into sleep to the sound of the northman's unending recitation, seemingly indifferent to the absence of an audience.

TWO

The Climb

"

AND, THOUGH SHE IMPLORED ME TO STAY at her side, I steeled my heart and returned to my uncle's ship, for bound by duty was I, and even the promise of a queen's love was insufficient to sway me …"

"Does he ever stop?" Shamil muttered to Lyvia as they clambered to the top of a craggy rock face, one of several they had traversed that morning, each time to the accompaniment of Tolveg's endless epic.

"When he finally gets to the part where he returns home," she replied with a wince. "And then he just starts over, and the story changes with every telling. His lovelorn queen was merely a countess last time."

Shamil had woken that morning to the stomach-teasing

scent of meat on the spit, finding Lyvia roasting a fresh-caught rabbit over the fire. Noble origins or not, she was no stranger to the wilds or the hunt. Her stern silence from the previous night abated somewhat once they had shared a meal and commenced the long climb to the Eyrie's summit, although they were obliged to converse during the all-too-brief respites from Tolveg's story.

"So you think it's all lies?" he asked her. They paused on a ledge, waiting for the others to catch up. He and Lyvia had quickly proven themselves as the most agile climbers, and it would have been easy to leave the two older men behind. This climb, however, was bound by an ancient custom that dictated they all arrive at the summit together.

"Possibly." Lyvia shrugged. "Though that sword certainly isn't just for show. I've seen enough warriors to know the face of one who's actually tasted battle." She frowned, lowering her face a little. "Unlike me."

"And me," Shamil admitted.

"Truly?" Her frown became puzzled as she nodded to the raptorile-tail whip on his belt. "I thought that must be a trophy. Your people war endlessly with the lizardfolk, do they not?"

Shamil's hand went to the whip, unwelcome memories rising as his fingers traced over the azure and emerald-hued scales that formed its base. *The eyes ... There was a soul behind its eyes ...*

"Just a gift," he said, swallowing a cough. Eager for a distraction he leant forward to offer a hand as Rignar clambered the final few feet to the ledge.

By Shamil's reckoning they had scaled near a third of the mountain by midday, their progress partially assisted by the pathway cut into the stone, presumably by the previous generations of sentinels. It wasn't much of a track, however, being frequently too narrow for easy navigation and often disappearing altogether at the base of yet another cliff face in need of climbing. The surrounding stone was often marked with various inscriptions, most of them carved in letters or glyphs beyond Shamil's comprehension, though both Lyvia and Rignar had little difficulty in providing a translation.

"'Loelle Estarik of Mira-Vielle,'" the mage read, his blunt fingers tracing over one inscription that appeared less weathered than the others. "'Second Wing of the Sentinel Eyrie. To my mother's shade I offer the most earnest contrition for my sin.'" He raised an eyebrow at Lyvia. "A country woman of yours, it seems."

"It's a famous scandal," she said, a shadow passing over her face as she surveyed the carved symbols. "She fell in love with a lord from a rival house and, at his urging, disclosed her family's treacherous scheming to win the throne. The entire family went to the gallows, save Loelle, who was allowed the mercy of exile and service in the Sentinels."

"Then perhaps she awaits us above," Shamil said, eyeing the winding and irksomely narrow trail ahead.

"I doubt it." Lyvia started forward with a faintly mocking grin. "Unless she's found a means of extending her life by two centuries. Plays have been written about her, none of them particularly good, it must be said."

Mention of theatre, unfortunately, provided yet another opening for Tolveg to regale them with more of his adventures, on the pretext that such high drama would surely one day attract the attention of a playwright.

"For it was with my words, not my sword, that I laid low the three-eyed reptile of the Black Fjord, famed for taking the form of a comely maiden in order to lure besotted sailors into her deadly embrace …"

The tale wore on for the remaining hours of daylight and much of the night that followed as they huddled in their cloaks and tried to sleep on a ledge no more than three feet wide. Once again Shamil drifted into a fitful slumber to the sound of Tolveg's voice only to awaken come the dawn to find he had begun the story all over again, only, this time the shapeshifting three-eyed reptile had become a water nymph of astonishing beauty.

"In the name of the four winds …" Shamil began through clenched teeth only for the words "shut up!" to die on his lips when Rignar clamped a firm hand to his shoulder. Meeting the mage's eyes, Shamil found an implacable command to silence and, as they flicked towards Tolveg, a measure of pity.

Shamil noticed it then: the small quiver to Tolveg's voice as he spoke, the way his hands would sometimes stray to the scars on his neck, trembling for a second before he snatched them away. This was a man filled with fear, a fear that could only be assuaged by the constant recitation of his own story, real or imagined as it may be.

So they shared a sparse meal of salted meat and resumed their climb without a word of protest as Tolveg's saga continued. He filled the next few hours with such contradictory constancy that, when he finally fell silent, Shamil found himself halting in surprise at the sudden absence of his voice.

They had scaled a steep, winding path to the mountain's eastward flank, finding a stiff, chill wind to greet them that held the sting of more than just the cold. Shamil's nostrils flared at the acrid, sulphurous taint to the air, eyes tracking to its obvious source half-a-dozen miles distant. The cloud rose in ugly billows of yellow and grey, shrouding much of the craggy ridgeline below, thinning periodically to reveal the gaping, circular fissure from which it poured.

"The Maw," Shamil murmured. Gazing upon something of such legendary status aroused a curious mix of emotions, from simple awe to a shameful sense of pride. With his own eyes he had beheld something few born to his homeland would ever see, but he had bought the experience at the cost of his honour. Throughout his trek north his mind had churned through various imaginings of what the Maw would actually look like, from a vast, bottomless pit to a jagged, flame-belching crack in the earth. Seeing the reality of it, he felt no sense of anticlimax, even though it amounted to just a very large hole spewing a good deal of foul smoke into the air. It was the reality of it that awed him, the inescapable fact that the entrance to the last refuge of the malign Voice actually existed. Furthermore, all other aspects of the legend were fully present.

The jagged teeth of the Smeldthorn Mountains lay beyond the smoke, their black slopes laced in veins of glowing red lava birthed by the many volcanoes in their midst. The veins came together to form a sluggish river of molten rock that flowed down the ridge before angling south, creating a steaming, pulsing barrier between the smoking rent of the Maw and the greener lands that formed the eastern frontier of the Treaty Realms. Despite the ugly spectacle of the scene, most of Shamil's attention was not captured by the Maw or the molten river but by the vast statue that rose from its eastern bank.

He put its height at close to five hundred feet, the granite from which it had been fashioned rendered black by centuries of smoke from the Maw. Shamil supposed this was fitting since the

woman it depicted was said to have worn dark armour throughout
her many battles. Sharrow-Met, the Great Redeemed Wraith
Queen, Founder and Saviour of the Treaty Realms, stood side-
on to the Maw, both arms resting on the pommel of her mighty
scimitar so that the giant edifice of woman and blade created
a huge arch of sorts. Her features, stern with either resolve or
perhaps disdain, had somehow escaped the blackening smoke and
so shone pale in comparison to the rest of her massive body. Also,
as Shamil's gaze tracked over the fine cheekbones and aquiline
nose, he noted they were disconcertingly familiar.

"Don't," Lyvia said as he turned towards her. Unlike the
statue, her features were weary rather than stern, mouth twisted
in an annoyed grimace. "I've been hearing it all my life. So,
please don't."

The expression she cast at the statue was reflective rather
than awed, proving a stark contrast to Rignar. The mage stared at
Sharrow-Met's stone effigy with unblinking eyes and face slack, as
if the sight of her had been sufficient to banish all other thought
from his head. Watching tears well in Rignar's eyes, Shamil was
reminded of something he had witnessed in boyhood, his aunt's
face the day his uncle returned from the last war against the
raptorile. It had been a long war, and his uncle was no warrior,
merely a potter called to serve his city at a time of direst need.
Seeing her face that day when the kitchen door opened to reveal
a smiling man in besmirched, dented armour, Shamil understood
that she had never truly expected him to return. It was the face
of a soul looking upon another that it loved absolutely.

Shamil found Tolveg's reaction to the sight of the statue
the most curious. He stood with his face turned away and arms
crossed, silent for once, but in a way that brought no sense of

relief. For when Shamil caught sight of his features, he saw only the terror the northman had been striving to contain throughout their journey.

"They say her battle mages built it in just three days," Lyvia said, drawing Shamil's attention back to the statue. "In their grief they joined their powers to raise up the stone and from it crafted a monument greater than all others, just to mark the place of her passing."

"Nonsense," Rignar muttered, blinking as he wiped at his eyes. "Building the statue required mage power, it's true, but it was still the work of years, not days. And she didn't die at the cusp of the Maw."

This differed from every tale Shamil had ever read or heard regarding Sharrow-Met's demise, placing Rignar at odds with a considerable body of scholarship and lore. However, the surety of his voice left little doubt that, at least in his own mind, he spoke the truth.

"Then where did she die?" Lyvia asked, her voice coloured by a caustic skepticism.

"No one knows." Rignar displayed no overt offence as, with obvious effort, he tore his gaze from the statue to resume the trek. "She suffered wounds in the last charge that drove the Voice's vile horde into the Maw, wounds that would surely have killed a lesser soul. All we know for sure is that, when the last arrow had fallen and the dust and smoke settled, she was gone."

"Set to wander the earth until our hour of direst need?" Lyvia asked, her tone taking on a taunting quality. "Are you a Revenantist, then? Is that why you're here?"

Rignar paused in the act of hauling himself up to the next ledge, his own tone one of sadness rather than resentment. "Revenantists are fanatics lost in a welter of delusion. I am not so fortunate, my lady." He inclined his head at the path awaiting them, a series of ever more narrow pathways that resembled a zig-zag pattern of scars slashed into the mountain's side. "Shall we?"

· ♦ ·

TOLVEG SAID NOTHING FOR THE REST OF THE DAY, SOME-thing for which Shamil should have been grateful. Instead, the warrior's silence soon began to stir an oppressive concern. He plodded at the rear of their party, his face set in a rigid mask, red-rimmed eyes distant, and offering only grunts to Shamil's forced attempts at conversation. He took comfort from the fact that they had surely scaled two thirds of the mountain's height by now and the Eyrie's summit lay only one more day's climb away. He knew enough not to expect complete safety upon reaching the Sentinels' holdfast, but the challenges that awaited them there at least offered the prospect of restitution, something they had all travelled a great distance to claim. When they saw the fire wing, however, any hope Shamil harboured that the prospect of reaching their destination would restore Tolveg's spirits dwindled and fluttered away on the mountain wind.

It swept out of a nearby cloud bank without warning, its shadow passing over them before their ears detected its passage through the air. Shamil was obliged to squint into the sun's glare to catch his first glimpse of the bird, watching the wings give a single mighty beat that sent it soaring high. Seeing it silhouetted against the cool blue of the mountain sky, Shamil felt a lurch in his heart at the sheer majesty of the beast, wings at least thirty paces from tip to tip, sunlight glittering through the feathers of its fanned tail, body the size of a warhorse.

As the bird angled its wings to sweep back towards them, Shamil was able to discern the bright colouring of its feathers, a mix of red and gold that gave the impression of flame as they caught the sun. Shortening its wings, the bird came straight towards them at a shallow angle, allowing Shamil to make out the smaller bulk of the sentinel perched on its back. His initial glance made him wonder if it might be another bizarre creation of nature, its head seemingly deformed into something that resembled a teardrop with two black eyes peering down at them in blank indifference as the eagle streaked overhead. *A helm*, Shamil realised, noting the bronze sheen of the teardrop and the straps holding it in place before the eagle banked away and disappeared into the cloud below.

The four of them stood in silent regard of the clouds until Lyvia coughed and said in a small voice, "Bigger than I thought it would be."

"Much," Shamil agreed, his head filled with visions of what it might be like to ride such a creature and finding to his surprise that they stirred more anticipation than dread.

"The fire wing is second only to the black wing in size," Rignar said. "And there are said to be hardly any of those left."

Tolveg said nothing, moving to the ledge to peer down at the drifting clouds. They had reached a comparatively broad stretch of track, even featuring a few steps cut into the stone but no wall that might prevent a climber from coming perilously close to a sheer drop.

"Tolveg," Shamil cautioned, seeing the tip of the northman's boot protrude over the edge, scattering gravel into the void.

"That's not my name," the blond warrior said in a soft voice. He raised his head as Shamil took a step towards him. He was gratified to see the man's terror had disappeared, his face now wearing a serene smile as his long locks trailed in the wind. "They took it from me, you see, the day they scourged me." His hand half rose towards his neck in an echo of his habitual gesture, then paused and fell to his side. "It's the law, the deserved fate of one who murders a kinsman. Tolveg Clearwater died, and in his place was Blood-Mad, murderer of uncles, worthy of only spit and curses."

Seeing Tolveg's other boot scrape towards the edge, Shamil took another tentative step forward. "I doubt names matter much in the Eyrie," he said, extending a hand.

"They seemed to think I wanted to do it," Tolveg went on, voice dimmed with puzzled recollection. "That I somehow lusted for my uncle's death, out of … envy, perhaps? But why? Why would they think that?"

"When we become sentinels, you'll prove them wrong." Shamil took another step, gauging the distance between them at little over three yards, too far to leap and catch him in time.

"But I had to." Tolveg's gaze froze Shamil in mid-step, the serenity abruptly replaced by a desperate need for understanding. "I begged him to stop. I begged him to turn the ship back. 'Have we not witnessed wonders enough, Uncle? Is our hold not crammed with treasure? But now it is always dark and the seas we sail bare of all save ice. Truly we have reached the limit of the world.' But turn back he wouldn't. He was well into his madness by then. Star-cursed my people call it, a soul lost to the lure of endless discovery. We sailed further north than any ship in all the sagas, and it still wasn't enough."

He sighed, and the desperation in his face faded into sorrowful acceptance. "He gave me this the day we set off." Tolveg's hands moved to the buckle of his sword belt, unclasping it from his hips. "*Alken-Haft*, a blade fit for only the hand of a hero, or so he said." Tolveg smiled as he hefted the sword and looked into Shamil's eyes. "And I can see that this is no place for cowards."

He threw the sword at Shamil, hard enough to force him to retreat a step so he could catch it, stopping the rune-etched pommel an inch from his nose. When Shamil lowered it, Tolveg was gone.

The Eyrie

"YOU COULD HAVE SAVED HIM."

Rignar glanced briefly at Shamil's stern, accusing visage before turning away, huddling into his cloak. "Leave it be, lad," he muttered.

The three of them had spent the hours until nightfall climbing in silence, eventually finding a resting place at the foot of a stone ladder cut into a sheer cliff some fifty feet high, too high and too narrow to scale in darkness. Throughout the climb Shamil had kept to the rear, hoping the mage could feel his eyes boring into the back of his skull. Shamil had seen death before, including the deaths of friends, for the Doctrinate's lessons held many dangers, but never had he witnessed a man casting his own life away, especially when such a waste could have been prevented.

"The pendant you carry has power," Shamil persisted. "*You* have power. You could have stopped his fall …"

"Some men are fated to die young," Rignar cut in, voice dull with fatigue. "Saving him wouldn't have changed that. Fear followed him like the stink that follows a drunkard, the fear that had cracked his mind when he murdered his uncle, the kind of fear that never fades. Better he spare others the cowardice that would surely have claimed him in battle."

"What do you know of battle?"

"More than you, my young friend. Since I've actually seen a few." Rignar shifted, letting out an irritated groan. "Best get some sleep. I've a sense tomorrow will be a hard trial for all of us."

But Shamil's mind was too full of Tolveg's serene smile to allow the comfort of sleep. He sat with his back against the first step, the northman's sword propped between his knees. He turned it continually, watching the light of the quarter moon play on the runes engraved on the pommel. There were more on the blade itself, a remarkable thing of beauty that demanded admiration, bright and keen, the edge possessing the slight irregularity that came from the grind of a whetstone over many years. It bore only a few scratches, leaving the symbols that marked it intact, not that he could read them.

"It'll be a battle ode to one of their many spirit gods."

Lyvia gathered her cloak about her as she sat up, the keenness of her eyes indicating a similar inability to sleep.

"Can you read it?" he asked, holding out the sword.

She shook her head, making no move to take the weapon. "No, but I know a little of the northmen's customs, one of which holds that touching another warrior's sword invites a dire curse."

"It's not mine."

"It is now. Tolveg's last act was to gift it to you, and I'm sure he had good reason, however cracked his mind might have been."

They both started as Rignar let out a sharp exhalation and shuddered in his sleep. Checking his face, Shamil saw that Rignar's eyes remained closed, but his features were drawn into a mask of deep distress. Shamil decided that the mage's dreams must be terrible indeed to visit him with so much pain and terror. Rignar's lips moved in a tremulous whisper, the words mostly gibberish but for a few sentences rendered near meaningless by archaic phrasing.

"... I beg of thee ...," the mage whimpered, face bunching in fresh alarm. "... Hearken to thine heart ... thou hast suffered enough ..."

Gradually, the words faded away, and Rignar calmed, his features slackening until snores replaced fearful whispers.

"He's been like this every night," Lyvia said. "Once Tolveg finally stopped talking and fell to slumber. You slept through it all."

"But you didn't."

She shrugged, looking away, her face becoming guarded. "I sleep little."

"You called him a Revenantist." Shamil looked again at Rignar's snoring features, thinking how unremarkable a figure he would have been but for the pendant he wore. "What is that?"

"A cult, popular in my city until recently." She angled her head, studying Rignar. "I doubt he's truly one of them, though. No fanatic was ever so cynical."

"This cult worshipped Sharrow-Met?"

"In a way. Their founder claimed to have received a vision of the redeemed Wraith Queen wandering the earth in revenant form, neither dead nor alive, in perpetual expectation of the day she'll be needed. 'When the Voice is once again heard in the Treaty Realms, the Wraith Queen will forsake her endless wandering and rise to be our salvation once more.'

"This self-proclaimed visionary made himself quite powerful for a time, rich too, until one of his more zealous adherents decided he was in fact a fraud and put a hefty dose of poison in his wine. The cult splintered in the aftermath, lingering on in factions that seem more interested in fighting each other than proclaiming Sharrow-Met's imminent return."

"Imminent return?"

"The heartlands of the Treaty Realms are troubled, at least more troubled than the normal course of history would dictate. Once-loyal kinsmen vie for power, harvests are poor, reports of plague and famine are rife. It's all fertile ground for any would-be prophet offering hope in the form of a long-dead legend. If she did ever deign to return, now would seem a very good time." Her voice slipped into a whisper, face clouding as she added, "The beggared and the dispossessed will unite to follow another queen ..."

She blinked and stiffened, turning away to lie down, pulling her cloak over her head. "You really should keep the sword, Shamil," she told him in a sigh. "I think Tolveg hoped you could use it to win the honour he could never regain."

· ♦ ·

THE WOMAN WAITING TO GREET THEM AT THE TOP OF the steps stood at least six feet tall, with copper-coloured hair bound in tight braids. She wore a fur cloak against the wind, which parted with the frequent gusts to reveal a leather harness covering a frame of lean muscle and, Shamil noted as he tried vainly not to let his eyes linger, more than a few scars. She gave no response to Rignar's panted greeting as they hauled themselves up the final step, her arms crossed in silent scrutiny. Her angular visage surveyed them each in turn, lingering briefly on Shamil, longer on Rignar, and longest of all on Lyvia. Her eyes narrowed in recognition as they roved the younger woman's face, a faintly puzzled line bisecting the scar on her brow.

"The resemblance has been remarked upon many times …" Lyvia began in a tired voice, only for the woman to bark out a harsh command.

"Shut your mouth, fledgling!" She glared at Lyvia for a moment longer, as if daring her to speak again, then grunted and turned to Rignar. "There were four of you yesterday," she stated.

"Our companion … fell," Rignar replied.

The woman's head tilted in slight acknowledgment before shifting to regard the steps they had climbed. "Do any others follow?"

"No." Rignar gave an apologetic smile. "It's just us."

Shamil saw the woman grimace before she turned away, staring up a path of wind-worn flagstones leading to a gateway in a wall a dozen feet high. "My name is Tihla Javahn, Second Wing of the Sentinel Eyrie," the woman said. She moved with a rapid stride their recent exertions made it hard to match, and her words held the dry and passionless tones of an oft-recited speech. "As fledgling sentinels, your training is in my hands. You will follow my instructions without question. If you do disobey, and such disobedience doesn't result in your death, you will depart this place and never come back. There is no negotiation here. There is no bargaining here. I care nothing for your excuses, explanations, or entreaties. Nor do I care about whatever disgrace brought you to this mountain top. Understand this and accept it, or leave now."

She came to a halt beneath the gate, turning to regard them with hard intent, her hand emerging from her cloak to hold up a brass disc. It was a thin, roughly worked thing, embossed with a crude silhouette of an eagle in flight. In material terms it possessed little value, but to Shamil it was worth all the wealth he would ever own.

"This is what you came for," Tihla Javahn told them. "The token that symbolises restored honour through service to the Sentinel Eyrie. It may take years to earn it, it may take months. Most likely you will die in pursuit of it. Stepping through this gate signifies your submission to the Eyrie, its customs, its rules, and the sacrifice required of its mission. Do not enter lightly."

She moved aside, inclining her head at what lay beyond the gate. Shamil stepped forward without hesitation, drawing up short at the sight of the Eyrie in its entirety. It was composed of stepped tiers carved from the summit of the mountain, creating a series of rises and dips. Wooden platforms had been constructed atop each rise, linked by a complex, overlapping maze of walkways. A dozen or more canvas-sailed windmills turned continuously in the stiff wind, and other sentinels moved about carrying various burdens. Most paused to regard the newcomers for a short examination, but none felt inclined to wave or call out a greeting.

Rising above the windmills were a number of thick poles, each as tall as an aged pine, featuring broad crossbeams. Their purpose soon became obvious when a huge shape swept out of the sky and flared its wings, talons the length of sabres reaching

out to grasp the perch. Shamil had thought the bird they had seen before Tolveg's fall to be the biggest he would ever see, but this creature was at least a third again as large. Its great beak parted to emit a piercing cry as it folded its wings, the feathers betraying a flame-like shimmer. The sentinel on its back un-hooked his harness from the straps about the fire wing's neck before leaping nimbly to catch hold of one of the ropes dangling from the crossbeam. A large man, his fur cloak parted to reveal a torso of thick muscle as he descended to the ground, his fall made gentle by a counterweight that swept up as he swept down.

He released the rope a few feet shy of the ground, landing on a slanted walkway and sliding to the nearest platform. He made his way towards the gate in a series of leaps and swings, pausing briefly to exchange greetings with other sentinels, all of whom smiled or nodded with notable deference. Upon landing he strode towards the newcomers, tugging thick leather gauntlets from his hands before unfastening the teardrop-shaped bronze helm from his head.

After Tihla's severity, Shamil was surprised to see a smiling visage as the helm came away. Based on his frame, Shamil would have guessed this man's age at somewhere in his thirties, but the face he revealed bore the creases and weathering of a much older man. As he halted, his lips parted to reveal a wall of white, apart from a single gold tooth gleaming bright in the sun.

"Fledgling sentinels," he said, bowing and speaking in a voice that was low but strong. "I bid you welcome to the Eyrie." His smile dimmed a fraction as he looked at the empty ground beyond the gate. "This is all?" he enquired of Tihla.

"There were four." She shrugged. "One fell."

"Ah." His face betrayed a short flicker of dismay before the smile returned in full measure. "No matter. All who brave the climb are welcome." He bowed again. "Morgath Durnholm, First Wing of the Sentinel Eyrie, thanks you for your selflessness in coming here."

Lyvia gave a visible start at the mention of the man's name and failed to match the bow Shamil offered the leader of the Sentinels. It was awkward and clumsy, as the custom was unknown in his homeland. Rignar also offered no bow, but did step forward to clasp the First Wing's hand.

"Rignar Banlufsson," he said. "I present my companions Shamil L'Estalt of Anverest and Lady Lyvia Gondarik of Mira-Vielle."

"No noble titles here," Tihla said, adding in a low mutter, "certainly no ladies."

Morgath Durnholm spared his second-in-command a reproachful arch of his eyebrow before turning back to Rignar. Shamil noted how his gaze barely lingered on Lyvia, as if forcing himself not to stare. "You're the crystal mage we've been expecting for so long," he said, pointing to the pendant about Rignar's neck. "Shelka, our last practitioner of the art, went to join with the spirits of her forebears last winter. She was very old and, despite having won her disc years ago, decided to live out her days amongst those she had come to see as family. For that is what we are." He smiled again, moving to rest a hand on each of their shoulders, his affability faltering somewhat when Lyvia took a pointed backward step, her face lowered and expression rigidly inexpressive.

Shamil found his shoulder sagging a little under the weight of the First Wing's hand, the fellow looming above him by several inches. However, any suspicion that his gesture might be an attempt to demonstrate superior strength was dispelled by the genuine warmth that glimmered in Morgath's eyes. Shamil had been trained to spot signs of deceit or hidden malice and saw none here.

"We have a good deal for you to do, Master Mage," the First Wing said, turning back to Rignar. "The Eyrie has a decent stock of crystals, but that will soon change in the event of another incursion."

"Is such a thing expected?" Rignar asked.

"The Maw is sparing in the signs and portents it provides. It could belch flame for a day, and yet the skies remain clear of its foul denizens, only for dozens to spew forth a fortnight later. I've often thought we could do with a seer in the Eyrie, but as yet none has felt sufficiently disgraced to join our family."

"They tend to be a solitary lot," Rignar agreed. "Disgrace is reserved for those of us who actually engage with the world."

"Ah yes, the world." Morgath's brows rose in faint interest. "How fares it?"

Rignar's face formed a humourless grimace. "Poorly. Not so many of the Treaty Realms still hold to ancient obligations, hence our number."

"Numbers aren't everything. I'd rather three stout hearts come in search of restored honour than a hundred souls forced to our door by mere obligation."

He smiled again, less broadly, before turning to Tihla, voice lowered. "I'll need to take Fleyrak for another patrol before nightfall. Saw an odd shadow in the smoke."

The Second Wing's scarred brow creased in concern. "Something new?"

"Or just a trick of the light. My eyes aren't what they were."

"I'll come with you."

"You have more pressing duties." He cast a meaningful glance at Shamil and the others. "I'll take Shirmar. He's fully healed now and keen to get back into the sky."

"Take Lamira too," she told him, her tone hard with insistence, before adding with a bland smile, "Her eyes are younger."

Morgath gave a brief laugh, then turned to bow to the three new arrivals a final time. "Tihla will see to your training. Throughout the days ahead it would be best to remind yourselves that what she does, she does for love of family."

He turned and walked away, leaving Tihla to regard them with a baleful eye. "Understand this," she said in very precise tones, "I do not love you. Mage." She beckoned Rignar forward, pointing to the western edge of the Eyrie where the carved tiers abruptly ended in a stretch of vertical rock. It was covered from base to crest in wooden scaffolding, the rock face featuring numerous circular, cave-like openings too regular of appearance to have been naturally formed. "Best if you take Shelka's old chamber. It's on the lowest tier, second from the left. She left behind a pile of books and trinkets you may find a use for. Get settled and join us to eat after dark. You'll go to the nest tomorrow. Better hope one likes you, or you've had a wasted journey."

Rignar hesitated, turning to regard Shamil and Lyvia. "I assumed I would be training with my friends ..."

"Mages don't train," Tihla interrupted. "Can't risk losing your talents. Apart from the leap, of course. No sentinel can avoid that."

Rignar gave a reluctant nod, forcing a smile at his younger companions. "Until tomorrow, then."

After he started for his new home, Tihla stood in silent

regard of her two charges, gaze roaming over their various weapons. "Know how to use that, do you?" she asked, gesturing to the strongbow slung across Shamil's shoulders.

"I do," he replied.

She blinked before her eyes slid to Lyvia, narrowing with a resentment Shamil assumed resulted from the disrespect the noblewoman had shown to the First Wing. "And you?" Tihla flicked a finger at the sling dangling from Lyvia's belt.

"All women of my house are trained in combat from a young age," Lyvia replied promptly. "Proficiency in weapons is considered as important as comportment and etiquette."

The edges of Tihla's mouth curved very slightly. "We'll see. For now"—she nodded to a stack of broad-bladed shovels resting near the gate—"you have a far more important task to perform."

FOUR

Fledglings

"**M**ORGATH DURNHOLM WAS THE MOST DREADED pirate in the entire history of the Treaty Realms."

Lyvia's words were muffled somewhat by the scarf she had fastened over her nose and mouth in an effort to assuage the stink, but Shamil detected the heat in her words, nonetheless.

"He didn't seem … piratical."

"What?"

Like her, he had covered his mouth so was obliged to pull down the black silk kerchief in order to repeat himself. "He didn't seem …" Shamil choked off as the miasma that filled the roofless channel immediately assailed his nostrils and throat. He coughed, fixing his kerchief back in place and shaking his head.

"They say he took over a hundred ships," she went on, grunting as she forced her shovel through a particularly stubborn mound. Once dislodged from the stone, it came apart to unleash a stench so thick they were forced to the tunnel mouth, retching and heaving clean air into their lungs. This end of the tunnel led to the south-facing flank of the mountain, ending abruptly in a sheer drop of dizzying depth, the stone below streaked with white and yellow from years of discarded effluent. They had learned over the course of the previous two days that seeking relief at the tunnel's other opening would earn only a rebuke from Tihla and a curt instruction to get back to work.

"He wasn't kind to the crews either," Lyvia continued in a gasp, slumping against the tunnel wall. "Dozens of sailors thrown to the tiger fish for his sadistic amusement. When the king's fleet finally caught him, it's said he spat in the admiral's face and demanded immediate execution."

"And yet here he is," Shamil pointed out. "Pirate no longer."

"It was the admiral that brought him here, in chains. The admiral's name was Argath Durnholm, you see." She gave an exasperated sigh at Shamil's puzzled expression. "His father. Morgath was ... is a renegade son to one of the great houses of Mira-Vielle. A man of even slightly less noble blood would have been subjected to the eighty cuts, and that's not a pleasant fate, let me tell you."

"When was this?"

"Oh, before I was born, twenty-something years ago or thereabouts. I really didn't expect to find him still alive, let alone First Wing of this place."

"And I didn't expect to spend my time shovelling this." Shamil cast a scrap of ordure through the opening with his shovel blade. "How many tons will it take to gain a disc, I wonder?"

Her response was drowned out by a piercing shriek that echoed through the tunnel with sufficient force to pain the ears. It was a regular occurrence, but Shamil doubted he would ever accustom himself to the calls of the mighty birds roosting in the great cavern above. So far, the only evidence they had seen of the creatures consisted of a few overlarge feathers and the steady but unpredictable arrival of the substance they had the dubious honour of clearing away. Worse than the effluent, however, were the bones. Most were the cracked or severed remnants of goats or sheep, but now and again they would unearth a skull of unfamiliar appearance. Most were too badly damaged to make out much of their features, but Shamil eventually found one that was mostly intact.

"Any notion of what this might be?" he asked Lyvia. They had paused to enjoy the benefit of a gust of wind from the southern end of the tunnel, an infrequent event that would banish the stink for a blessed moment or two.

He crouched to retrieve the skull from a dried mound of droppings, the yellow ash falling away to reveal what at first glance he might have taken for the skull of a child. The rounded crown of the head was roughly human in shape, but the resemblance disappeared when he turned it to examine the face. Two overlarge eye sockets regarded him above narrow nostrils and a set of misaligned, jagged teeth. Each tooth was the length of a coffin nail and still sharp, as he discovered to his cost upon touching a finger to the tip of the most prominent one. It was a small tap, but blood swelled immediately from the pinprick wound, soon followed by a sharp pain more acute than seemed natural.

"Something from the Maw, I expect," Lyvia said. She eyed the skull with a dark wariness and, unlike Shamil, showed no inclination to touch it.

"It's a flenser."

They both turned to find Tihla standing in the tunnel, surveying the results of their work with a critical eye.

"Body like a monkey with wings like a bat. The teeth, though." She shook her head with a humourless laugh, eyes still roving the newly scraped tunnel. "One bite is usually enough to kill, and if it doesn't, their drool is so loaded with foulness the wound will fester so fast you'll be dead in a day. One of the Maw's less dangerous children."

She sniffed, head tilting in faint satisfaction. "Stink's not so bad now. Should hold us for another few weeks. Stow your shovels by the gate and fetch your weapons. Time to find out if you two were bragging."

◆ ◆ ◆

SHAMIL'S FEET SKIDDED A FEW INCHES ALONG THE PILlar's summit as he landed, arms windmilling briefly to regain his balance. Once steadied, he unslung his bow and nocked an arrow, raising the weapon to loose at the target suspended from a rope a dozen feet above his head. He watched the shaft slam into the centre of the wooden circle, then turned, smoothly nocking another arrow to the string, then loosing at the target to his right, scoring another perfect hit. Crouching, he fixed his gaze on the neighbouring pillar, forcing himself not to dwell on the thicket of thorn bushes below. It was a ten-foot drop, but Shamil feared the thorns more than the fall.

He leapt, this time achieving a less solid landing. One foot slipped as it connected with the pillar's marble top, flailing in the air for the brief second or two it took Shamil to find his balance once more. Fortunately, his next pair of arrows were just as

well aimed as the first, the wooden targets swaying as the shafts found their mark. His accuracy, however, failed to stir any appreciation from Tihla when he hopped from the sixth and final pillar to land at her side.

"Too slow," she said. "Next time don't stop to admire your handiwork." She jerked her head at Lyvia. "Get to it, fledgling."

After they had retrieved their weapons from their shared chamber, the Second Wing had led them to the northern flank of the Eyrie where a semicircle of marble pillars rose from a thick mass of thorn bushes surrounding the base of a tall mound of tiered rock. Above the pillars wooden targets dangled from a web of ropes.

"Every battle fought by a sentinel takes place in the air," Tihla told them. "The fear of falling is ingrained in every one of us, as well it should be, but to fight from a greatwing's back requires that you master that fear. Your path lies before you." She gestured to the pillars. "Built here and abandoned centuries ago by hands unknown. The thorn bushes we planted ourselves, a reminder to fledglings that falling has consequences." As evidence she raised her forearm to display a pale, jagged scar tracing from her wrist to her elbow. "My first and last fall. The thorn cut so deep Shelka had to use her crystals to seal it else I'd have bled to death." She fixed them with a smile that didn't touch her eyes. "Is your mage friend so skilled at healing, I wonder?"

When Lyvia's turn came she proved to be swifter than Shamil, leaping on nimble feet to linger on the first pillar just long enough to whirl her sling and cast a stone at the nearest target. Her aim wasn't as true as his, however, the stone smacking into the target's edge and sending it spinning. Unlike Shamil, Lyvia took Tihla's words to heart and didn't loiter to watch.

Slipping another stone into her sling, she whirled it and leapt again, unleashing the projectile in midair before twisting to land on the next pillar.

Shamil's admiration turned to alarm when he saw her lead foot connect with the edge of the pillar's crown rather than the flat surface. Lyvia twisted again as her foot skidded along the edge, trying to latch a hand onto the pillar before gravity did its work. She was only partially successful, managing to clamp one hand to the marble with enough of a grip to arrest her fall. Seeing how her straining fingers inched closer to the edge as she dangled, feet kicking in an ineffectual attempt to gain leverage on the pillar's upper stones, Shamil knew she had only seconds before plummeting into the possibly lethal embrace of the thorns.

He acted without thinking, casting his bow aside and leaping onto the first pillar, snatching the raptorile-tail whip from his belt. As he flicked his arm, it made a familiar, ear-straining crack, louder, it was said, than any other whip in all the Treaty Realms. The whip uncoiled like a deceptively lazy snake to wrap itself around Lyvia's waist just as her fingers lost their grip.

Although she wasn't a person of particular bulk, the suddenness of her fall made it impossible for him to haul her back up. Instead, he swung her, grunting with the effort of heaving the whip and its burden, Lyvia missing the thorns by bare inches. He let go at the midpoint of the swing, Lyvia landing hard on the bare stone a few yards from the thicket. She tumbled a short distance before coming to a halt, winded and groaning. As she looked up at Shamil, he was surprised to find a face that was pale with the shock of recent danger but also drawn in gratitude rather than injured pride.

Tihla's reaction was similarly unexpected, pursing her lips in approval rather than anger as she watched Lyvia untangle herself from Shamil's whip. Instead of voicing an acerbic injunction against saving fledglings from their deserved injuries, she nodded to Lyvia untangling herself from the whip. "An impressive instrument," the Second Wing observed. "I assume it can kill as well as save?"

"I have a steel barb for the tip," Shamil confirmed. "If need arises."

"Need will surely arise, so be sure to keep it sharp." She cupped her hands around her mouth to call down to Lyvia. "Stop lazing about and get back up here, fledgling! Try again, and ponder the folly of overconfidence whilst you're at it."

• ♦ •

THE NEXT TWO WEEKS FOLLOWED A DAILY ROUTINE OF enlivening training and soul-taxing drudgery. Mornings were spent at the pillars, Tihla hectoring them to ever increasing speed. Shamil came close to falling only once more whilst Lyvia's initial mishap seemed to have birthed a near manic concentration that ensured an uncanny sure-footedness. Within a few days she could hop from one pillar to another without the slightest pause, sling whirling all the while as stones thunked against the targets in a rapid drumbeat. Shamil quickly resigned himself to not matching her speed, although Tihla seemed satisfied with his progress and reserved the bulk of her criticism for the less dangerous but more arduous aspects of their training.

"Duck, you cack-brain!" she snarled, swinging the spear again, this time at his chest instead of his head. The weapon was called a claw spear and was at least twice the length of any pole-arm Shamil had encountered before. The haft was fashioned from ash, which allowed it to flex as Tihla wielded it, aiming the curved point at the upper parts of his body. The spearhead consisted of a black claw fixed to the haft by an iron bracket. This particular claw had a leather sheath to prevent its serrated edge from tearing his flesh, but the sting of its impact was a thing to be feared, and he bore several long, crescent-shaped bruises on his back from his first abortive practice.

The spearpoint whooshed within an inch of his head as he sprawled flat, then sprang to his feet and dodged back to avoid the next swing. Tihla was far from done, however, grunting as she brought the spear around, then up, bringing it down in a hammer blow that would surely have cracked his skull had he not dived clear in time.

The spear haft broke as the point connected with the ground, the leather sheath coming away due to the force of the impact. The revealed claw was black as obsidian, catching a narrow gleam along its curve and glimmers on the jagged serrations.

"It's from a scyther," Tihla explained. "It's a despoiled breed of condor, twice the size, with plenty of vicious cunning. Luckily, we only see a few each year, and they tend to fly alone." She cast an annoyed eye at the broken spear haft before tossing it to Shamil. "Enough for today. Take this to Ehlias to get fixed, then do five circuits around the rises. I'll be watching, so no slacking."

◆ ♦ ◆

SHAMIL ASSUMED THAT EHLIAS KEHN ARNDSTVEL, METAL smith to the Eyrie, must have once possessed hair much the same as Tolveg's, given that they hailed from the same realm. If so, there was no evidence of long golden locks on the pink-

and-purple globe of his head, nor even the smallest hair as far as Shamil could tell. There seemed to be scarcely an inch of his broad, muscle-thick frame that hadn't received either a scorch or a burn severe enough to discolour or pucker the skin. His face was further testament to a life rich in injury, one milky white eye stared out from a socket crisscrossed by deep rents in the surrounding flesh. Despite it all, Shamil found him the most cheerful soul in the Eyrie, his voice raised in unending song as he worked, often providing a counterpoint to the ringing toll of his hammer on the anvil.

His songs were all voiced in the language of his homeland, making them meaningless to Shamil's ear. Even so, he was able to discern the underlying theme from the smith's tone, for his voice was a fine and pure thing, capable of conveying great sorrow as well as joy. Today the tune was sombre, mournful notes accompanying the rasp of his file on a newly crafted knife. Shamil found himself pausing at the circular doorway to the smith's chamber, captured by the smith's melody as it summoned Tolveg's face to mind, the serene, acceptance just before he jumped.

"Broken another one, has she?"

Ehlias set his tools aside to come forward and relieve him of the spear. "A hefty blow," Shamil said, handing the weapon over. "I was fortunate to avoid it."

"She's always had a strong arm, that one." Ehlias's good eye surveyed the broken haft and spearpoint in careful appraisal before adding both to a stack of weapons and gear in the corner of his workshop. "Tell her it'll take me a day or two. Got a whole bundle of arrows to prepare for the new mage's crystals."

"I will." Shamil turned to go but found himself dithering in the doorway, one hand fidgeting on the sword at his belt.

"Something else?" the smith asked.

"Yes a … personal matter." Shamil unbuckled his sword belt and extended the sheathed weapon to Ehlias. "There are runes on the blade. I was wondering if you could tell me what they mean." The smith's usually affable visage slipped into something far more stern, but also riven with a reluctant curiosity that deepened as he came closer to peer at the sword's hilt and pommel. "Show me," he said, making no move to take the sword.

Shamil drew the blade from the sheath, placing it on a nearby bench. Ehlias surveyed the runes in narrow-eyed silence for some time before telling Shamil to turn it over. "Where'd you get this, lad?" he asked after a similarly prolonged scrutiny of the reversed blade.

"It was given to me by a fellow exile during the climb. He … fell."

"No he didn't. Not if he gave this willingly into another's hand. Do you have any notion of what this is?"

"I thought it just a sword, better crafted than most and pleasing to the eye, to be sure. But still, just a sword."

Ehlias let out a soft sigh as his finger, still not touching the steel, traced the runes on one half of the blade. "These are signs of the stars my people look to for guidance on the seas, and in life. These"—his finger shifted to the markings on the opposite side—"are the names of the smiths who crafted this sword, and no ordinary smiths were they. Truth be told, I never thought to see one of these in my time upon this earth." He stepped back from the bench, shaking his head before fixing Shamil with a serious, intent gaze. "It's a *skeln-blad*. A fated blade, forged by steel-mages and given only to those destined to perform great deeds."

"Its owner did murder and went mad," Shamil replied in bafflement. "It's why he was exiled. Although, he did tell a great many stories of impressive deeds. But how many were true ..."

"If any of these deeds fulfilled the purpose this blade was crafted for, he'd have held fast to it when he threw himself from the mountain. No warrior of the Wodewehl would forsake the chance to carry such a potent weapon into the eternal battles of the Hidden Realms. Instead, he gave it to you. You're its owner now, lad. Seems a great deal is expected of you."

Shamil began to object further, but stilled his tongue in the face of the smith's steady-eyed certainty. "Do the runes say what it is?" he asked, nodding to the blade. "This great purpose?"

Ehlias smoothed a hand over his motley scalp, disfigured brows bunching into a web as he pondered for a moment. "Those who crafted it named it *Alken-Haft*," he said. "Which means Ice Cutter. So ..." He gave a forced, apologetic smile. "If I were you, I'd have a care when winter comes, for it falls hard in these mountains."

◆ ♦ ◆

SPEAR PRACTICE WAS FOLLOWED BY AN HOUR SPENT traversing the network of walkways and ropes that covered the Eyrie. Most of the sentinels flew away on their birds to patrol the afternoon skies until dusk, creating an empty playground through which Shamil and Lyvia would sprint and leap, always trying to complete a circuit faster than the previous attempt. The wisdom of this particular lesson was twofold and obvious; they quickly gained an intimate understanding of their new home whilst also developing muscle and stamina.

Shamil found it a pleasing contrast to the Doctrinate, where the lessons could often be tedious, if not pointless. Whilst he learned a great deal about combat in his years within its walls, the Doctrinate was as much a temple as a school, and students would spend days memorising ancient lore in dead languages only to be punished for minor grammatical mistakes when called upon to recite it. The Eyrie was not bound by such meaningless custom. Here all lessons were pared down to the necessary skills of a sentinel, although Tihla had yet to even make mention of the one he ached most to learn.

"They don't speak to them," he observed to Lyvia one evening. It had become their habit to spend the brief respite after traversing the Eyrie atop one of the taller platforms, where they could watch the sentinels returning from their patrols. "The riders don't talk to the birds," he elaborated in response to Lyvia's frown. "So how do they control them?"

He pointed to where Shirmar, a veteran of brawny build whose skin bore almost as many scars as Ehlias's, guided his fire wing to a perch. The bird shortened its wings as it glided through the forest of poles to alight on the one closest to Shirmar's chamber, all done without a shout from the rider on its back.

"One of Sharrow-Met's final acts was to bind all the great-wing breeds to the Sentinels," Lyvia replied. "Or so it's said. When one dies, another arrives within days, be it an owl, a blue falcon or a fire wing. Somehow they know to send one of their number in accordance with the Wraith Queen's wishes. As for their riders, I'm not sure who controls whom. Supposedly the bond between bird and sentinel allows for a depth of understanding beyond the ken of mage or scholar."

"If they choose you," Shamil pointed out in a low murmur. "And don't decide to let you fall."

His eyes slipped to the nest, the tallest rise in the Eyrie, a narrow spike of rock beneath which they had laboured to clear the ordure of the creatures that nested in its upper reaches. Within waited birds who had yet to accept a rider, one of which he hoped would choose him before the day of the leap finally dawned.

"I saw Rignar this morning," Lyvia said, her tone deliberately bright, he assumed in an effort to alleviate his doubts. "Seems he's already bonded with his bird, an owl he calls Kritzlasch. Mages are always bonded to owls, apparently."

Shamil gave a vague nod in response, gaze still locked on the nest. "It would seem appropriate."

"Some legends have it that the birds see into your soul. If they find courage, they choose you." She nudged him with a hard shove of her boot. "In which case, I think you worry over nothing."

Shamil glanced at her half-smiling, half-annoyed face before looking away, as unwanted memories rose for the first time since his arrival at the Eyrie.

The raptorile blinked its eyes, and he saw the soul behind them, saw its pain and fear, saw that it felt and thought as he did … saw enough to suffer the weakness that disgraced him.

"Yes," he muttered back, getting to his feet. "I heard the same thing. Come, Tihla will be expecting us at the spit."

FIVE

Stielbek

OME EVENING, THE SENTINELS WOULD GATHER IN the bowl-shaped nexus of channels between the tiered rises. When the sky began to darken, it fell to the fledglings to roast either a goat or a boar over the glowing coals piled into a circular pit, a chore that required regular and attentive turning of the spit. They were also required to boil and stir the vegetable broth in large iron bowls, which served as an accompaniment to the feast of meat. Shamil found this the most onerous of their chores, requiring over three hours of labour amidst air steamed to an oppressive, sweat-inducing thickness. Tihla had issued stern instructions that they remain silent throughout these nightly gatherings, and they were permitted to eat only after the sentinels had had their fill.

At first, Shamil had expected some measure of taunting and ridicule from these veterans, such things being a salient and required feature of life in the Doctrinate; his back still bore the marks of stones and various projectiles hurled at him by the older students along with a torrent of verbal abuse. But no bullying was forthcoming, instead the two fledglings were either ignored or spared a rare glance of sympathy or grim encouragement.

The assembly numbered about a hundred in all, and Shamil saw no unscarred faces amongst them, several sporting eye patches, whilst a few wore wrought-iron hooks in place of lost hands or wooden pegs instead of vanished legs. He therefore found the good humour that pervaded the gathering distinctly odd, even jarring. Men and women with injuries that would have seen them beggared in most realms exchanged affectionate jibes and roared with laughter at ribald jokes. Tales of near death and calamity abounded but were never spoken in dire or foreboding tones. He might have ascribed it to the forced bravado found amongst many a warrior band, but the absence of fear in this place was as potent as the sense of warm companionship. Morgath Durnholm had spoken true, this really was a family.

The First Wing spoke often throughout the evening, but Shamil noticed he never shared any stories of his own, instead commenting on the various tales with observations that were either gently chiding or concealed a compliment within apparent scorn. Durnholm was also, Shamil saw with growing admiration, highly skilled at quelling the rare disagreements or burgeoning arguments that rose amongst his subordinates. Sometimes two sentinels would carry mismatched memories of an event, which could lead to conflict for it was clear that a correct accounting of shared history was highly important in the Eyrie.

"No," one stated, interrupting a lurid recounting of the death of a comrade some years before. She was a slender woman of similar complexion to Shamil but spoke with an unfamiliar accent, coloured now by an emphatic note as she rose, shaking her head at the stocky storyteller opposite. "It wasn't just flensers that day. There was a whole company of vehlgard archers at the lip of the Maw too. That's why Hawber took his bird so high. That flenser pack would never have got him otherwise."

"He soared high because he was too fond of flying, Ashinta," the stocky man returned, not without good humour, but also with a steely defiance in his eye. "Sky mad. Something we should all guard against."

"He was no more sky mad than I," Ashinta insisted, voice growing heated enough to draw a glower from the storyteller. His face darkened as his lips began to form a response, the retort lost when Morgath's voice rang out, loud and cheery.

"We're all sky mad!" he laughed, rising to clap a hand to Ashinta's shoulder. "At least a little. Else, why would be here?"

This drew a laugh from the other sentinels, and just like that the rising tension was gone. Morgath Durnholm, it seemed, knew how to wield his words as well as Tihla could wield a spear. Ashinta gave a slightly sheepish grin as the First Wing jostled her, resuming her seat whilst he raised his voice once more.

"I think, brothers and sisters, our fledglings have endured our tales long enough." He turned, extending a hand to Shamil and Lyvia. They were busily scouring slops from the pots and took a moment to realise all eyes were now turned in their direction.

"Fourteen evenings filled with stories of enough horror to send any sane soul scrambling down this mountain," Morgath went on, eyes warm as he regarded them, "and yet they stayed.

Despite every indignity, chore, and injury our excellent Second Wing heaped upon them, they stayed. She has pronounced them ready for the choosing, and I agree. Do I hear a dissenting voice?"

There was a long moment of silence, Shamil's gaze tracking over the tiers of serious faces arrayed on all sides, finding shrewd appraisal on some but acceptance on most. The silence stretched until Morgath gave a satisfied nod, only for a single voice to speak up.

"The girl," Ashinta said, dark eyes fixed on Lyvia. "She looks too much like the Wraith Queen's statue. It's … unnerving. An ill omen, some might think."

"Are you a seer now?" another sentinel asked, sending a ripple of amusement through the crowd.

"Course I'm cacking not!" The woman's snarl faded into a grimace as she continued to stare at Lyvia. "Just worried how the birds will take to her is all. Mine gets twitchy at the mere sight of her."

"The greatwings will decide," Morgath told her, his voice for once devoid of humour and possessing a note of authority that caused Ashinta to meet his eyes. "The Eyrie belongs to them as much as us. She'll be chosen, or she won't. Besides, none of us can help how we look." He held her gaze until she nodded and looked away.

"Then it's decided." The First Wing moved to wrap a broad arm around Shamil and Lyvia, pulling them close. Shamil noted that this time his fellow fledgling didn't shrink from the First Wing's touch. "Tomorrow, our young friends will meet the greatwings, and let's hope they emerge with all their fingers intact!"

He laughed, long and loud, and the collective amusement of the sentinels filled the bowl and cast their mirth into the night sky like a roar. As it faded, Shamil saw a blossom of red above the Eyrie's eastern flank, brief and gone in an instant, but very bright, nonetheless. No one else, however, seemed to notice.

· ♦ ·

THE ODOUR EMANATING FROM THE CONICAL PEAK OF the nest was not so unpleasant as the stench of the tunnel beneath, but still brought a wrinkle to Shamil's nose. It was rich in raw meat, as he would have expected, but also bore the taint of breath exhaled by inhuman lungs.

"Right," Tihla said, dumping the sack containing a recently butchered goat at the entrance. Getting there had required a confusing climb of a dozen crisscrossed ladders made arduous by the burden of meat they had to carry. "Best if you spend no more than an hour feeding them at first; they'll get scratchy otherwise. When you're done, report to Ehlias. Time you two got fitted for your helmets." With that Tihla started back down the ladder.

"We don't need to be ..." Lyvia began uncertainly, "... introduced?"

This provoked a short laugh from the Second Wing as she continued her descent. "Rest assured, they'll introduce themselves," she said before her head disappeared from view, "if they like you."

"And if they don't?" Lyvia called after her, receiving no reply apart from the sound of Tihla leaping to grasp a nearby rope swing.

Shamil and Lyvia exchanged an uneasy glance before turning to the dark oval of the entrance. As yet, none of the birds within had felt the need to call out, but the two could hear the rustle of feathers and the scrape of talons on stone or wood.

"I shan't take offence if you wish to precede me through this doorway," Lyvia murmured. "Terrible breach of etiquette though it would be."

Shamil grunted a resigned laugh and bent to retrieve the sack Tihla had dumped, hefting it alongside the one already on his shoulder before taking a breath and stepping into the gloom. At first, he could see only an overlapping matrix of slanted sunlight streaming through the numerous openings in the nest's flanks. Motes and fragments of feathers drifted from dark to light, swirling when one of the unseen birds twitched its wings. Shamil progressed along a wooden walkway for a dozen paces before it opened into a wide circular platform. A loud fluttering of wings and swirl of displaced air told of birds alighting onto perches in the surrounding gloom. Still, it took the space of several laboured heartbeats before he caught his first close-up glimpse of a greatwing.

Two points of light glittered in the gloom to the side of the platform, joined by the thin curve of a gleaming beak as the bird bobbed its head. Shamil made out the red-gold sheen of its crest before it slipped back into the gloom, beak snapping in what he read as an impatient gesture.

Unslinging the sacks, he set one close to the platform's edge, drawing back the canvas to reveal the meat within. The bird's head flashed out of the gloom, snapping up a large chunk of goat haunch before fading back into the shadows. Soon there came the sound of tearing flesh and the dull wet grunt of food being gobbled down an eager throat. The only expression of gratitude or appreciation came in the form of a high-pitched screech and a gust of wind as the bird took flight. Shamil looked up in time to see the broad shadow flicker through the cat's cradle of light before it flashed through an opening and into the sky beyond.

Hearing a chorus of snapping beaks on all sides, Shamil set down his other sack and began to empty out the contents of both, distributing the hefty morsels of flesh evenly around the edge of the platform as Lyvia did the same. Sharp beaks darted from the darkness in a flurry, Shamil counting perhaps two dozen, seeing mostly the shimmer of red-and-gold plumage but also the occasional flash of blue or brown. Most seemed intent only on feeding, taking to wing when they had gobbled their fill, but a few would pause to cast an eye at the two human newcomers. None, however, seemed inclined to linger for more than a second or two of scrutiny, and Shamil was forced to ponder just how he would ever form a bond with any of these creatures.

"Oh, hello."

Turning, he saw Lyvia face-to-face with a bird that had hopped onto the platform's thick oakwood railing, head tilted at an inquisitive angle. Although smaller than the fire wings, with plumage of blue flecked with emerald green, it still stood three times the size of the woman who raised a tentative hand to touch its beak. Shamil began to shout a warning but stopped when he saw the bird still its head, shuddering a little at Lyvia's touch but not drawing back. From the faint click of contentment that emerged from the blue falcon's throat, it was abundantly clear that Ashinta's worries were unfounded. This greatwing at least saw nothing to fear in one who so closely resembled the long-vanished Wraith Queen.

"Aren't you beautiful," Lyvia told the falcon, smoothing her hand along its beak, receiving another appreciative click in response. "What's your name, I wonder?"

The bird lowered its head, allowing Lyvia to play a hand

through the short feathers of its crest, letting out a small, contented chirp that abruptly turned to a squawk of alarm as a very large shadow covered the platform from end to end. The blue falcon immediately hopped about and launched itself into the shadows, a massed drumbeat of wings and subsequent whirlwind of colliding air indicating the other birds had followed suit. Shamil's gaze snapped up to see a broad black silhouette, growing swiftly to obscure the slatted sunlight. The platform shuddered as the shape completed its descent, the impact sufficient to send Shamil and Lyvia staggering against the rails.

Shamil's gaze fixed on the bird's talons first, scythe blades of jet that had stabbed all the way through the platform's timbers. His gaze tracked upwards over the grey flesh of its legs to the feathers covering its chest, all as black as the talons, before settling on the bird's face. But for the gleam on its eyes and beak, it would have been indistinguishable from the shadows, forcing an inevitable conclusion.

"A black wing," Shamil breathed, taking a tentative step closer.

"I thought they were all gone," Lyvia breathed back. "Not seen in the Treaty Realms since the Wraith Queen's time. Shamil," she added, voice hard with warning as he continued to approach the huge bird.

"It's all right," he said, taking another step, finding himself captured by the sheer majesty of this beast. It towered over him, larger even than the mighty fire wing that carried Morgath Durnholm. The bird displayed no trepidation at his approach, merely tilting its head, eyes blinking white then black as a membrane slid over the shiny half spheres. As he neared, Shamil saw numerous scratches in the black wing's beak, though its point and edges

shone sharp in the meagre illumination. He also saw furrows in the plumage around the bird's mouth and eyes, glimpsing the pale, puckered flesh of long-healed scars beneath. This, he knew, was an old creature and no stranger to battle.

He came to a halt when the black wing abruptly bent its legs, lowering its body to peer directly at Shamil's face. It shifted from side to side with a slow, even grace he might have termed gentle but for the hard inquisition he saw in its gaze, the calculation behind the eyes born of something far from human. The rush of recognition brought a gasp to his lips, making him stiffen as the memory flashed bright and ugly in his mind.

The raptorile tried to raise itself from the sand, a hiss of pain escaping the long row of clenched, pointed teeth that lined its jaws. The wounds Shamil had inflicted upon it were too severe, however, and it collapsed, raising a pall of dust that soon cleared to reveal a defeated foe. Its eye rolled up to regard Shamil as he stepped closer, daggers raised for the killing strokes to the throat, the final act of this drama that would herald his graduation from the Doctrinate. Today, he became an anointed warrior of Anverest. All the years of pain and degradation, every blow suffered, and hard lesson beaten into his soul had led to this. He raised his daggers, looked into the defeated raptorile's eye, and stopped ...

The memory shattered, and breath exploded from Shamil's mouth, feet dragging on the timbers for several yards before he found himself on his back, gasping for air. A hard, concentrated pain throbbed in the centre of his chest, reminiscent of the ache left by a punch but magnified tenfold.

"Stop!" Lyvia shouted. Shamil craned his neck to see her rush to stand between him and the black wing, arms raised in warning. From the way it ignored her, Shamil deduced the bird saw no more threat in Lyvia than it would in a mouse, instead shifting to stare at his prostrate form with the same depth of scrutiny.

Groaning, Shamil rolled onto his side, dragged air into his lungs, and pushed himself to his feet. "Quite an introduction," he said through gritted teeth, stumbling towards the bird. "My name is Shamil L'Estalt." He performed a stiff parody of Morgath's bow, wincing and fighting the urge to cough up his breakfast. "Pleased to meet you."

The black wing angled his head to peer at Shamil with one eye, blinked, then launched itself into the air, the beat of its sail-like wings sending them both to their knees. Silence reigned for several seconds until the clack of beaks and rustling of feathers told of a semblance of calm returning to the nest. The black wing had departed this place, and none of the other greatwings were sorry for his parting.

"I think …" Shamil grunted after trying and failing to stand back up, "… he liked me."

∙ ✦ ∙

"SO, YOU MET STIELBEK."

Tihla squinted at the livid vertical bruise on Shamil's bared chest, lips pursed in consideration as she poked a finger to the purple flesh, provoking a shudder of suppressed pain. "Little bit harder and he'd have shattered your sternum. Must've caught him in a good mood."

"If you don't mind," Rignar said with polite but firm insistence, causing the Second Wing to move aside. "This won't hurt," the mage told Shamil, holding a stone close to his bruise. The stone was smooth and deep red in colour, its hue starting to shift as Rignar channeled its power, flecks of blue light flaring to life in its facets. "Carnelian always works best for bruises."

Shamil's pain faded with sufficient suddenness to bring a surprised gasp to his lips, the bruise quickly losing its dark lividity to subside into a pinkish brown. Lyvia had helped him navigate the first few ladders as they climbed down from the nest, their progress slow and painful until Ashinta, freshly returned from patrol, noticed their plight. Her bird, a fire wing with more gold than red to its crest, swooped down to pluck him from the scaffolding, carrying him the short distance to Rignar's dwelling, where he was deposited at the door with unexpected gentleness.

Before flying off to her perch, the sentinel paused to look down at him, face hidden by her helm but the pity in her voice still audible as she said, "Don't take the leap, boy. If the birds don't take to you, there's nothing you can do. Best climb down and seek your honour elsewhere."

"I thought they were extinct," Shamil said, forcing his gaze from the fast-disappearing bruise. "The black wings."

"Could be he's the only one left," Tihla replied. "No sentinel's seen another for many a year. He turns up every time new fledglings climb the mountain, never chooses any, and flies off again. It's been going on since long before I got here, and that was fifteen summers ago."

"The black wings were known to nest far to the east," Rignar said, brow furrowed in concentration as he continued to hold the stone to Shamil's injury. "Appearing over the lands that became the Treaty Realms only rarely, and spreading terror when they did. Sharrow-Met formed an alliance with them with the aid of the Voice's dark magics, though many legends would have it that they followed her out of love rather than enchanted enslavement."

"Or love of slaughter," Tihla said. "Stielbek's a vicious swine.

Damn near took my head off when I first ventured into the nest."

"That should do it." Rignar said. The red stone's shimmer faded as the mage stood back from Shamil's chest, the bruise's colour now almost completely vanished, along with the pain.

"What about the others?" Tihla asked.

"We fed them." He shrugged and pulled on his shirt. "They ate the meat happily enough. A blue falcon seemed to take a liking to Lyvia."

"And you." Tihla's face took on a serious cast. "Did any take a liking to you?"

"Time was short before the black wing arrived."

She gave a short nod. "Go back tomorrow. Spend more time in their company. I doubt Stielbek will show up again now he's done his mischief for the year."

She turned to Rignar with a forced smile. "The First Wing would like news of your progress, Master Mage." She pointedly shifted her gaze to the baskets full of crystals lining one wall of his chamber. Shamil was no expert in such things, but he knew enough to recognise most as quartz with an occasional yellow gleam that told of topaz.

"It's coming," Rignar replied, and Shamil detected an undercurrent of irritation beneath his affable tone. "Better quality stone would make it go faster."

"This is what we have. It is a requirement of a sentinel's lot to make the best of the meagre resources the Treaty Realms choose to provide." Tihla's false smile broadened a fraction before disappearing completely. "Please, work faster." She moved to the doorway, glancing back at Shamil. "You don't need to cook tonight. Get some rest and be sure to return to the nest at first light."

After she departed, Rignar raised a caustic eyebrow at Shamil but made no other comment, moving to one of the baskets to grasp a handful of stones. "Once," he said with a wistful sigh, "I worked with only the highest-quality gems. Now"—his tone soured as he let the pale fragments of quartz fall back onto the pile—"I have these."

"Don't they work?" Shamil asked. "With your"—he waved a vague hand at Rignar, —"magical gifts."

"Magical gifts, eh?" Rignar repeated, lips quirking in amusement. "Tell me, my young friend, what do you know of crystalmancy?"

"Next to nothing," Shamil admitted, inclining his head as he rubbed a hand to his chest. "But I do appreciate it nonetheless."

"I think"—Rignar paused to reach for his cloak—"it's time you had a proper education in the subject. Besides"—he took a hammer and chisel from the row of tools above his workbench, placing them in a satchel, which he handed to Shamil—"there's a small task you can help me with, if you don't mind a little hard work."

The Black Onyx

"**L**ONG HAVE MAGES PONDERED THE ENIGMA AT the heart of crystalmancy," Rignar said in a tone that reminded Shamil of Lore Mistress Ishala, without doubt his favourite tutor at the Doctrinate. "Why should it be that such varied and potent energies arise from mere inanimate stone?"

Despite his interest in what the mage had to say, Shamil found himself continually distracted by the perilousness of their course, straining to listen whilst simultaneously inching his way along a ledge perhaps eight inches wide at its broadest point. "I don't see any steps or handholds around," he said, quelling a surge of panic when his foot dislodged a stone from the ledge, sending it tumbling into the misty void below. "The sentinels don't come here often, I assume."

"Even today," Rignar continued, ignoring the comment and making his own cautious but steady progress towards a flat outcrop of rock ahead, "no one is entirely sure of the fundamentals of the art. One thing is clear, however, facets are the key."

"Facets?" Shamil flattened himself against the cliff face as another sideways step sent a scattering of pebbles cascading into the clouds. "How so?"

"Complexity. The inner composition of every crystal is a matrix of flaws and channels far beyond the ability of any mortal mind to comprehend in full. I believe it is this complexity that lies at the heart of crystalmancy. Somehow"—Rignar grunted as he hauled himself from the ledge to the outcrop, turning to offer Shamil a hand—"those of us who possess this particular form of mage gift can channel it through these endlessly complex but tiny labyrinths to produce the desired effects."

"So"—Shamil took a firm grip, wrist to wrist, before levering himself to Rignar's side—"the magic doesn't reside in the stones? They are a conduit rather than a source?"

"That, my friend, brings us to a philosophical debate that has raged amongst mages for centuries. And to illustrate, I have a present for you."

Rignar fished in his satchel to retrieve what at first appeared to be a trinket fashioned from one of the many fragments of white quartz in his chamber. As Rignar placed it in his hand, Shamil saw that the stone had been chiseled into a rough cylinder and fixed to an iron cap with copper wire. Looking closer, he also saw faint tendrils of light within the stone, much like in the carnelian the mage had used to heal him.

"I currently spend perhaps six hours a day making these, along with various other deadly instruments," Rignar said. "I think you can spare an arrow for a demonstration, don't you?"

Shamil nodded as understanding dawned, unslinging his bow and taking an arrow from his quiver. He used his dagger to snip off the arrowhead and fitted the quartz fragment in its place, twisting the copper wire to tie it to the shaft. "I'll need a target," he told Rignar, nocking the arrow to his bowstring.

"Oh, that'll do, I think." The mage pointed to a jut of rock some thirty yards away, from which a small tree sprouted. Shamil drew the strongbow's string to his lips, sighting on the tree, then pulled back the final few inches until the heel of his palm brushed his ear before letting fly. The arrow's flight was straight and fast, Shamil reflexively raising his arm to cover his face when a bright, violent explosion obscured the tree and the rock it stood on. Scant smoke accompanied the blast, just a white circle of expanding light that blinked out of existence almost as soon as it appeared, leaving a cascade of shattered rock and a blackened, leafless tree in its wake.

"Power enough to kill three men contained within a crystal no bigger than my thumb," Rignar commented. "The power to destroy and the power to heal. The essential contradiction at the heart of crystalmancy."

Lowering his bow, Shamil experienced a pang of regret at visiting destruction on something that had contrived to flourish despite the unfriendly climate found at such a height.

"Trees are hardy," Rignar said, reading the thoughts on Shamil's face. "Don't worry; he'll grow back, probably stronger than before. Here"—his hand disappeared into the satchel again, coming out with a larger trinket, this one fashioned from a triangular piece of yellow topaz set into a silver clasp—"another gift, for your whip."

"Doesn't explode, does it?" Shamil asked, regarding the item with a dubious eye as Rignar handed it over.

"No. But it would be best to exercise due care when using it."

Shamil unfurled his whip, fixing the device to the tip with the clasp. As he swirled the handle in preparation for an experimental strike, he noticed Rignar take a long backward step, raising a hand to shield his eyes. Grinding his jaw in mixed trepidation and irresistible curiosity, Shamil drew the whip back, then up and round, causing it to lash with cobra-like speed. The topaz tip flared as the whip reached its maximum length, birthing a ball of shimmering light that resembled a cage fashioned from lightning bolts. It faded along with the echo of the whip's crack, leaving an unfamiliar taint to the air that for some reason put Shamil in mind of the sea.

"When propelled to sufficient velocity," Rignar explained, "magically infused topaz releases a particular form of energy potent enough to burn the very air and separate it into its constituent gases."

"Potent enough to kill?" Shamil enquired, coiling up the whip and peering at the crystal tip. The topaz seemed to have suffered no injury, although there were a few black smears on the silver clasp.

"A man, certainly. As for the fearful creations spewed forth by the Maw …" Rignar trialed off, glancing over his shoulder at the smoking spectacle of the great orifice beyond Sharrow-Met's statue. "Well, if they're fashioned from flesh, then it will surely do them injury, or at least cause some severe annoyance."

"My thanks," Shamil told him in sincere appreciation, returning the whip to his belt. "For an excellent and powerful gift, one I doubt I'll ever be able to return in kind. But I confess I fail to see how exploding arrowheads and energetic topaz relate to your philosophical quandary."

"Because they inevitably lead to a singular and important question: Did I unlock such power from within the crystals or place it there? I suspect the latter, but many of my fellow mages insist on the former, quite passionately too. Crystalmancy, they argue, requires no inherent knowledge on the part of the wielder. You can be as ignorant as a stump and still craft a stone capable of blowing your head off if you're not careful; therefore, the magic must lie in stone not body or soul."

He fell silent, eyes narrowed as he surveyed the sheer face of the cliff above. "Ah," he said, pointing. "There it is. I knew it couldn't be far away." He moved to the cliff face and began to climb, rapidly scaling several feet and moving with a fluent surety that told of a familiarity with this corner of the mountain.

"You've been exploring, I see," Shamil observed as he found a handhold and began to follow the mage's course.

"No," Rignar replied. "Never been here before. It's the mountain, lad. It speaks to me." He paused to smooth a hand over the granite, and Shamil saw the glitter of tiny crystals in the stone. "Clear as any map."

"Wouldn't that contradict your argument? If the stone possesses the power to guide you, doesn't that mean the magic resides within it rather than you?"

"A fair point. I can see your education included logic as well as archery. But it stems from an unproven assertion that the stones possess some form of agency, some desire to guide me to my goal. Whereas I, as a being possessed of reason, may be utilising my gift to call upon knowledge contained within the crystals in this mountain. Knowledge and power may equate as a metaphor, but not in the literal sense."

Shamil came to a halt, feeling a brain-stretching ache behind his eyes that begged for a change of subject. "Speaking of goals," he said, resuming the climb, "what exactly are we looking for?"

Rignar didn't answer immediately, speaking only when he had climbed to the lip of a horizontal crack in the cliff face. "Something I was told to find," he muttered. "Though a part of me hopes we never do."

With that he climbed into the crack and disappeared. Following, Shamil discovered that what had appeared to be a narrow crack in the mountainside was in fact a cave mouth. Inside, Shamil found himself in a cramped and dark hollow dribbled by rivulets of water from some hidden spring. He could see little until a blue glow flared into life, illuminating the sight of Rignar with a shimmering crystal in his hand. The mage muttered to himself as he moved about the cave, eyes scouring every inch of rock.

"I could help," Shamil said, "if I had some notion of what to look for."

Rignar barely seemed to hear, replying with a vague shake of his head. "Smooth as sun-kissed ice, black as a raven's eye ..." he murmured, continuing his survey without pause, the shining crystal he held painting the uneven stone in a shifting collage of bizarre shadows.

"Is this why you chose to become a sentinel?" Shamil persisted. "Just to find this thing, whatever it is?"

"Choose?" Rignar said, coming to a halt, voice riven with amused bitterness. "All my choices were made for me long ago, lad ..." His voice died as his eyes alighted on something in the cave's floor. Crouching, he lowered his crystal to allow the light to play on something that contrasted with the surrounding rock in the clean, narrow gleam it caught from the glowing stone.

"Onyx." Rignar's voice was soft as he traced a finger over the smooth surface of his discovery. "Black onyx to be precise. But bigger than I've ever seen before." His gaze snapped to Shamil, a thin but triumphant smile on his lips. "Time to pay me back for those gifts, my young friend, with sweat."

◆ ◆ ◆

CHIPPING AWAY ENOUGH STONE TO FREE THE ONYX FROM its granite prison would have required many hours, perhaps days of labour if Shamil's efforts with hammer and chisel hadn't been augmented by Rignar's magics. Taking an apple-sized piece of dark grey rock from his satchel, he played it over the stone surrounding the onyx. It emitted no light, but Shamil heard a dull thrum followed by a harsh, grinding hiss and multiple dust plumes as a web of cracks appeared in the granite.

"Lodestone," Rignar explained, returning it to his satchel. "I once brought down a castle wall with one of these. Have at it, if you please."

A quarter hour of chipping and scraping away displaced rock was all that was needed to free the onyx, revealed as an irregular sphere about the size of a man's head. Its smooth, unscarred surface was veined with silvery white swirls that glowed as Rignar extended a hand to it, a hand that trembled before the mage clamped it into a fist and drew it back.

"What is this?" Shamil asked him, disturbed by the fear he saw on Rignar's face. Suddenly, the mage appeared far older than his years, his bearded features sagging and a deep, sorrowful weight dulling his eyes.

"Something I was told to find, as I said," he replied in a preoccupied mutter.

"Told by who?"

Rignar's eyes flicked up at Shamil before shifting to focus on something beyond his shoulder. "I think you know."

Turning to regard the great statue rising above the wreaths of smoke, Shamil let out a sigh of realisation. "Sharrow-Met." He recalled the mage's fascination with Lyvia at their first meeting, the sense of a man looking upon a ghost. Then there were the fitful nightmares on the mountain when he would speak in archaic riddles. "You believe she speaks to you. In your dreams."

"Believe?" Rignar voiced a short, caustic laugh. "You think me deranged, don't you? Beset by delusions that have led me all the way to the Eyrie on a madman's quest. No, Shamil, I don't believe it. I *know* it. And they aren't dreams. I'd call them nightmares, except they're real. I don't just witness them, I live them, as she did. I wasn't much older than you the first time it happened, young, cocksure, arrogant in my power and greedy with it. It wasn't a pleasant combination. I had a valuable gift, one I barely understood but fully intended to sell only to those who could pay, and pay well."

He lowered his gaze to the onyx, extending a finger to hover within an inch of the surface, the silver veins pulsing white in response. "I was quick to forsake the chilly, feud-riven land of my birth when the mage gift rose in me, journeying south and finding a lucrative niche for myself in the port cities to the west. Opal, like lodestone, amethyst, and onyx, is an element stone, one that can exert power over water, enough to quell fractious waves and see ships safely to harbour, along with their very valuable cargoes. I only had to sell a dozen stones before merchants were beating down my door with fat purses in hand. It didn't take long before I became rather wealthy. A mansion in every port, all the fine wine and food I could eat. Years of indulgence made me rather fat, it must be said, but since I had fine carriages to take me wherever I wished, it didn't matter. But a rich man can swiftly become poor when fate comes knocking."

His face clouded as he continued to stare at the stone, shadows rising and falling on the creases of his face as the glowing veins pulsed. Shamil watched Rignar's hand grasp the emerald pendant dangling from his neck, holding it up with a rueful arch of his brows.

"Ignorant as a stump," he said. "That was me in my greedy youth. I bought this from a travelling dealer in gems, as I was always keen to add to my collection. I knew emerald was linked to the mind somehow but didn't fully comprehend just how. It's a singularly alarming thing to go sink yourself into a large and very soft bed only to wake up and find yourself in the midst of one of the bloodiest battles in all history. Memory, you see? That's what emerald holds, and this one had sat around the neck of a long-dead fellow who had the misfortune to witness Sharrow-Met's final victory over the Voice, fought only a few miles from this very mountain.

"I saw it all, Shamil. The combined armies of the Treaty Realms surging like a mighty wave against the Voice's malign horde. Suffice to say, it didn't look like any of the paintings, tapestries, or murals would have you believe. War is all ugliness, and glory is a lie we tell ourselves so we keep coming back for more. I heard the screams of thousands, smelt the blood and the filth that rises from sundered flesh, saw as much terror and grief as I did fury and courage. It would have been enough to drive me mad, had I not also seen her."

Rignar paused, the spectre of a smile passing over his face. "She, at least, the paintings tend to get right, in the sheer majesty of her if not the details. Even then, I've never seen one that really does her justice. In all respects she was worthy of her legend, sweeping low over the ranks of the horde on the back of her black wing, the great bird's talons reaping as terrible a harvest as her famed black scimitar. Despite the slaughter, I thought her the most beautiful sight I ever beheld. And she saw me. Impossible as it seems, as her black wing swept up and turned, she looked down from its back and looked directly into my eyes ..."

He trailed off into a grimace. "I woke screaming that night, casting the emerald away, determined never to wear it again. I locked it away in a chest and spent many months travelling, buying opals, imbuing them with power, and selling them to eager customers. So industrious was I, it's said my efforts alone were responsible for making the western ports the richest cities in the known world. But it was all a vain effort to smother the vision, quell the ever-growing temptation to unlock the chest and don the pendant once more, see *her* once more. And, of course, like any true addict, eventually I did.

"The next time was different. No battle, no slaughter, just a barren, flat plain scoured by a hard wind. She was shorn of her armour and clad in furs, though she still wore the scimitar on her back. She was alone but for the unseen man whose mind I had momentarily stolen, but a screech from above and a passing shadow on the earth told me her black wing hadn't forsaken her. She smiled as she looked into my eyes and said, 'So, thou hast returned. We should talk, I and thee.'"

He fell to silence, setting his satchel down and carefully

reaching to gather up the onyx, the veins flaring brighter still at his touch.

"And what did you talk of?" Shamil prompted.

"Oh, many things over the years." Rignar placed the onyx in his satchel before rising, hefting the strap across his shoulders. "Things that made me abandon my life of greed and embark upon a very long road that eventually brought me here, to find this." He patted the satchel, then moved to the cave mouth, crouching to begin the climb down. "Time we got back, I think."

"But why?" Shamil persisted, hurrying to follow. "What for?"

"The same thing that brought you here: a desire for restored honour." Rignar began his descent with much the same fluency as his ascent, swiftly disappearing from sight and forcing Shamil to scramble in pursuit.

"How does seeing Sharrow-Met in your dreams dishonour you?" he pressed. "I would have thought the opposite would be true."

"The things she told me led me to many places and many acts. All of them necessary but not all of them admirable. I have stolen, lied, cheated …" Rignar fell silent, Shamil glancing down to see him paused in mid-climb, his balding head lowered. "And killed, all in service to words told to me by a woman who lived four centuries ago. Perhaps"—he let out a humourless laugh as he resumed his descent—"you're right, and I am mad after all."

"But her words were true." Shamil leapt clear of the cliff as they neared the base, landing on the outcrop at Rignar's side. "They led you to the onyx. There must be a reason."

The mage regarded him in silence, his expression a mix of subdued amusement and apologetic regret. "Of course," he replied eventually, shrugging. "But telling you won't change what will happen here. Nor make it any easier." He stepped towards the ledge, then stopped as Shamil moved into his path, arms crossed and face stern with insistent resolve.

"Make what easier?" he demanded. "What is going to happen here?"

Rignar's sigh was that of a weary but indulgent parent who couldn't be bothered to spank a defiant child. "The legends are at least partly true regarding the sentinels. At least in the manner of their founding. Sharrow-Met did create them and call upon the greatwings to provide them with allies in the centuries to come. Their purpose has always been to contain the vile issue of the Maw, but their very existence conceals a darker truth: Sharrow-Met failed. She defeated the Voice's malign horde and drove it into the bowels of the earth, but the Voice persisted. She told me she wasn't even certain it could be destroyed, and so created the Sentinels to contain it whilst she began a quest to discover the means of ensuring its ultimate defeat. A quest, it transpires, that proved either fruitless or endless."

"So it's true? She still walks the earth?"

Rignar shook his head, lips forming a sad smile. "I don't know. Our conversations take place on that empty plain and nowhere else. It took her months to traverse it, even with her black wing's help, and every night she would camp and talk to me via the mind of the man who travelled with her. For years the visions have only repeated what she has told me before, revealing nothing of her fate, what she found beyond that plain. I know she went in search of the remnants of the immortals, the undying beings said to have once held dominion over the earth entire. 'From their seed did the Voice first rise,' she said. But traces of the immortals are rare, their stories too ancient and wreathed in myth to even be called history. Perhaps she really will return one day, but I find it … unlikely. She isn't coming to save us. I think she suspected that would be the case and so in me found a means to contest the Voice when it finally rose again."

"The Voice will rise again? She was sure of this?"

Rignar glanced over his shoulder at the smoke-shrouded statue and endless plume of yellow-grey foulness leaking from the Maw. "'As long as there be malice in the world, so will the Voice contrive to persist.' Those were the last words she said to me at the end of her trek across the plain. If she spoke true, I think we've both seen enough of this world to know that the Voice may have grown stronger than ever."

SEVEN

The Leap

T HE HELMS EHLIAS ISSUED TO SHAMIL AND LYVIA
were a testament to the smith's skills in that each was a
perfect fit despite being constructed purely by eye. They
weighed less than Shamil had expected but still possessed a decent heft, the weight distributed evenly between the elongated
blade that extended two feet from the rear of the helm and the
brass-and-copper mask that comprised the visor. This protruded
several inches in front of the wearer's face to accommodate three
sets of lenses.

"First is just plain glass," the smith explained. "Half an inch
thick so it'll guard your eyes from any claws that come stabbing.
Flick the lever on the side to switch to the next."

Shamil duly pressed a finger to the curved piece of iron

on the side of the helmet and found himself confronted by the irregular and colourful mass of an old burn mark on Ehlias's forehead.

"Fine-ground curved glass," he said. "Gives you about three times the sight you'd normally have. Can't match the birds, of course, but it might let you see a Maw beast before it gets close enough to sink its teeth into your throat. Good for spotting vehlgard on the ground too."

The third set of lenses rendered the smith's workshop a shadowy alcove of deep shadows, transforming the glimmer of his oil lamp into a faint pinprick of light. "Powdered obsidian mixed into standard glass when it's melted," Ehlias said. "Protects the eyes from blinding light, and it can get awful bright when the crystal-heads start flying."

They had only an hour to accustom themselves to the helms before Tihla came to ask them a question that had become a daily ritual after their fourth visit to the nest. Shamil had expected some measure of satisfaction, perhaps even a small glimmer of pride, when he gave his answer only to receive a frown of deep skepticism in response.

"You ready?" the Second Wing asked. "There's no doubt?"

Shamil didn't allow his gaze to linger on Tihla's frown, replying with a firm nod and as much certainty as he could muster. "Kaitlahr now accepts food from my hand and has allowed me to touch him. I feel the bond."

"Enough to name him, apparently."

"Yes. It means 'golden storm' in the ancient tongue of my homeland ..."

"I don't care what it means, fledgling. Neither does your bird. Naming them is our custom, one we adopted long ago, but only when we're sure they've accepted us as riders." She stepped closer, brow creasing further. "There's no shame in waiting," she told him, voice pitched far below her usual stridency. "Build the bond over weeks, months if that's what it takes, if it's truly there. The leap is not to be taken lightly. If you fall, you *fall*, and you've seen the bones of those that judged this wrong."

Shamil's hesitation was brief, but he knew she saw it. The bird he had named Kaitlahr was the same huge but youthful fire wing that had consented to accept his offered meat during his first foray into the nest. In truth, it was the only bird that continued to do so, and despite his claims, Shamil felt no real connection to the creature. He saw occasional glimmers of scrutiny in Kaitlahr's eyes, and he hadn't lied when he said the bird had allowed him a touch, but only once and for no more than a second before flaring its wings and launching itself into the gloomy recesses of the nest. Nevertheless, he clung to the notion that the fire wing had accepted him and would do what was required when he leapt. Rignar's words had left little doubt in his mind that his chance to win his disc would shortly arrive, and the prospect of failing to grasp it held more terrors even than the leap.

"He accepts me," Shamil insisted. "It's time."

He felt Lyvia shift at his side, a brief fidget of discomfort he assumed came from biting down contradictory words. She had been with him during every visit to the nest, the blue falcon she had befriended perched close to the entrance in eager anticipation of her arrival, whilst Shamil considered himself fortunate if Kaitlahr deigned to snatch meat from his hand.

"And you?" Tihla turned to Lyvia. "Named your falcon yet?"

"Vintress," Lyvia replied promptly. "'North wind' in the elder script." She paused to shoot an uncertain glance at Shamil, which he ignored. "We are also ready," Lyvia said, straightening.

"All right, then. I'll tell the mage and the First Wing." Tihla swept a hand through her tight braids, a rare expression of uncertainty that did much to stir the roiling in Shamil's stomach.

"Be there at noon." Both he and Lyvia were unable to contain a flinch of surprise as the Second Wing forced a smiled onto her lips. "Give you time to settle anything that needs settling."

She turned and strode off without another word, leaving a thick silence in her wake, which Lyvia eventually broke in a careful, hesitant tone.

"Shamil …"

"No!" he said, voice flat and hard as he walked away. "I'm ready. It's time."

•♦•

THE BEAM THEY WOULD LEAP FROM WAS TWELVE FEET long and aligned so that it pointed directly at Sharrow-Met's statue. Shamil found himself grateful for this as it gave his eyes something to fix on instead of straying continually to the ground far below. It was a clear day, and the space between summit and earth was for once free of clouds, allowing an uninterrupted view of what awaited him. He had heard that it was common for those who found themselves falling from great heights to expire out of fright before ever hitting the bottom and harboured a fervent if doubtful hope that it might be true.

Before addressing the gathered sentinels, Morgath Durnholm walked to the end of the beam with as confident a stride as if he were mere inches from the ground. When he spoke, it was in a booming voice full of grave authority, the kind of voice

Shamil knew had once commanded ships to terrible deeds in distant seas.

"Four centuries ago," the First Wing called out, "this band was founded by the redeemed Wraith Queen herself. Here she ordained a place of service where even the most wretched and disgraced could come to regain their honour. And what honour we have won, my friends. What battles we have fought. None of us came here with clean hands, certainly not I, but never did I witness the face of true evil until I came to the Eyrie. For there," his finger lanced out to stab at the Maw, "lurks the purest malice, the greatest threat to all that is good in this world. Our duty is a sacred one that requires the utmost commitment, for we do not serve here alone. Our service requires alliance with the greatwings, for without them our sacred duty cannot be fulfilled. Their trust was won long ago and must be maintained by every soul who seeks restored honour in our ranks. Today, three new fledglings come to win that trust, and I, as First Wing of the Sentinel Eyrie, profess myself humbled by their act."

He fell silent to an appreciative murmur from the other sentinels. Shamil had noted during the nightly gatherings that they were not a group given to overt displays of emotion or acclaim, but still, he took comfort from the many encouraging and approving glances turned his way.

"Tihla," Morgath said, extending a hand to the Second Wing. "Sound the horn!"

Tihla duly raised a large, curved horn derived from some huge beast beyond Shamil's experience. Putting it to her lips, she blew a long, grinding note that echoed around the Eyrie until an answering chorus came from the nest. The greatwings emerged from the many portals in a rush, screeching out their response to the summons as they swooped down. Shamil felt a fresh lurch in his gut at seeing Kaitlahr amongst them, flying alongside Vintress.

The birds angled their wings to form a circling flock a dozen yards above the beam, their cries dying away to herald the descent of a palpable hush. Shamil saw the encouragement fade from the faces of the sentinels as the silence persisted, replaced by the closed tension of those who had seen death many times and expected to see it again shortly.

"Rignar Banlufsson!" Morgath called out, striding from the beam to the cliff top. "Come forward!"

Rignar stirred at Shamil's side, pausing to grasp his shoulder, a frown of resigned determination on his brow, before making his way to the beam. Morgath held up a hand when Rignar placed his foot on the timber, speaking in a quieter but no less purposeful tone.

"Know that even now you may choose to step away. Your service will still be welcome here, bird or no."

Rignar nodded with a grimace of thanks, then buckled on his helm and took a deliberate step onto the beam. His progress along its length was far less confident than Morgath's, moving with his arms outstretched to maintain his balance and eyes locked firmly ahead. Reaching the end, the mage straightened, raising his face to the sky, chest swelling as he drew in a deep, shuddering breath. Then he leapt.

The owl that caught him moved so fast Rignar's salvation had been secured before he fell more than a few feet. The bird he had named Kritzlasch folded its wings to plummet down, voicing a screech as its talons enfolded the mage. It bore him up with a few beats of its wings, depositing him none too gently on one of the tiered rises before coming to rest on the tall perch sprouting from its summit. Rignar got unsteadily to his feet, raising a hand in a tremulous wave that drew a short-lived laugh from the sentinels.

"We welcome Rignar Banlufsson, Master Mage, to the ranks of the Sentinel Eyrie!" Morgath called out before turning to the two younger fledglings. "Lyvia Gondarik, come forward!"

Lyvia hesitated before walking to the beam, but Shamil saw no fear in her, only concern. "Please," she whispered, leaning close to him. "Don't do this."

Turning away she strode to the beam and nodded her way impatiently through Morgath's final warning before making smooth, unfaltering progress from the cliff to the beam's tip. Her face was a picture of serenity as she donned her helm, spread her arms, and toppled into the void.

Vintress shot from the circle of birds in a blur of blue, catching Lyvia just as her feet slipped from the beam. The falcon twisted, depositing Lyvia onto her back and letting out a cry that pained the ears in its joyful triumph. Instead of bearing Lyvia to one of the perches, Vintress swept back up to rejoin the whirling spiral of greatwings.

"We welcome Lyvia Gondarik to the ranks of the Sentinel Eyrie!" Morgath proclaimed, voice fading and gaze taking on a severe cast as he turned it on the last remaining fledgling. "Shamil L'Estalt, come forward!"

Shamil had thought this moment would be shorn of terror, his fears quelled by the depth of his determination. However, it was on weak legs and with a thumping heart that he approached the beam. He listened to Morgath's final warning with sweat beading his brow and soaking his back, the First Wing's words seemingly spoken from a very great distance; a vague, meaning-less echo.

"Not all are destined to rediscover their honour amongst our ranks ... There are many troubled corners of the world where so stout and skilled a warrior could redeem himself ..."

Shamil stood as still as his traitorous legs would allow, wait-ing for Morgath to fall silent, his gaze tracking from the beam to the far-off statue and back again.

"Young man." Morgath's grip bit hard into his shoulder, commanding his attention. "This is not a game ..."

"I know!" Shamil cut in. He spoke in a harsh, defiant growl, anger burning its way through his terror. Anger at Morgath for the effortless authority he commanded, at Tihla for the harsh indifference of her tutelage, at Rignar for his riddles, and shame-fully, at Lyvia for the ease with which she had won her bird's trust. Ever since his disgrace at the Doctrinate, it seemed the world contrived to deny him everything, and now this pirate turned peerless leader would refuse him even the chance of a decent end.

"A death suffered in search of honour is itself honourable," Shamil added, turning away. They were words spoken by Lore Mistress Ishala, a small, stooped old woman with eyes misted into blindness by age. Behind them lay a memory crammed with all the history her long life had allowed her to accrue. It was from her that he had learned of the Eyrie, and it had been her who pointed him on this sojourn. *Disgrace such as yours is the worst kind,* she had told him, lips formed into a kind but sad smile, *for it comes from within, not without, and I know of only one place in this world where such a curse can be lifted ...*

"If I can't be redeemed in battle," he said, straightening his back, "I'll be redeemed in death."

"No." Morgath's features took on a sorrowful cast, as he stepped back and his hand slipped from Shamil's shoulder. "Death is just death, son. It's what you leave behind that matters."

Despite his evident reluctance, the First Wing made no effort to stop Shamil as he walked to the end of the beam and raised his eyes to the swirl of birds above. He found Kaitlahr easily, the fire wing's silhouette was the largest amongst the throng and, Shamil saw in a welter of hope, flying below the others. Many thoughts flickered through his mind as he lowered his gaze to the great statue rising from the smoke in the distance: the faces of the aunt and uncle who had raised him, the stone monuments to the parents slain in the raptor-wars when he was barely out of the cradle, the many hardships and occasional triumphs of life in the Doctrinate, but most of all …

… *it's eyes stared up at him as he raised his blades, eyes full of knowledge that shouldn't be there, eyes that dimmed as he brought the daggers down, striking true, striking deep …*

Shamil leapt, not the arms-wide fall of Rignar or Lyvia, but a true leap. His legs propelled him from the beam, and he turned in the air, gazing up at the circling birds, a circle that shrank far more quickly than he had thought possible, the greatwings continuing to whirl in serene disregard of the human plummeting below. Before the circle became just a vague smudge against the pale blue of the sky, he fancied he saw Kaitlahr swoop lower, but it may have been just a final imagined flare of hope from a mind only seconds from death.

All the air rushed from Shamil's lungs in an instant as something slammed into his side. The world disappeared into a sudden reddish haze as he attempted to breathe, finding his chest too tightly gripped to allow it. He had time to reflect on the oddness of the ground impacting his side rather than his back before full blackness descended.

EIGHT

The Voice Awakened

H E WOKE GASPING. SWEET, CHILLY AIR FLOODED his throat and lungs, birthing a peculiar kind of ecstasy unique to survival. Tears rendered his vision a liquid blur of blue and black that cleared as he wept, shame and relief rising in equal measure. When the last tear fell, he found himself staring at the pale oval of Lyvia's face.

"I'm sorry," she said. "I had to."

She sat close to him on a ledge he recognised from their ascent to the Eyrie, Shamil guessing they were about halfway to the bottom. Vintress was perched on an outcrop some yards away, beak and talons busily rending a goat carcass to pieces. Lyvia coughed when he gave no response, forcing a weak smile as she turned to her bird. "She's so fast. Hard to believe a living creature could move so swiftly …"

"You should have let me fall." He spoke in a flat tone, lacking accusation or force, but still, he saw how deep the words stung her.

"I couldn't …" She shivered, hugging herself tight, keeping her gaze averted. "I've seen too many friends die, Shamil. Stood and watched and did nothing as they were led to the gallows, one by one. All my friends. Girls I laughed with when we played as children, gossiped with as we grew older. Boys I bickered with constantly and, as childhood faded, would sometimes kiss, only to bicker even more."

A smile of fond recollection passed over her face, but it faded quickly. "They all died," she went on. "And I watched, standing at my family's side on the balcony overlooking the great square in Mira-Vielle, even though I was just as guilty as they. I watched them all die the traitor's death. I told you some of it before, but not all.

"The Revenantist cult rose and fell, as I said, but its fall birthed an idea amongst the nobility's youth. We were a commendably earnest lot in some respects, filled with righteous anger at our families and their endless hoarding of power and wealth. Of course, some amongst us revelled in their privilege, whilst others hearkened to our expensive lessons and the many books we read. There was a boy …" She lowered her face, her expression alternating between the sadness and remembered joy Shamil knew came only from recalling a lost love. "A young man, Crucio. My young man, in fact. He was the only person I met who had read more books than I, and the only one who looked upon this face and saw more than just the image of a vanished legend. He burned with a need for change, a desire to sweep away the corruption and inequality that surrounded us. We would feed the poor, give succour to the sick and the helpless, but to do that we would need to learn from the success and failures of the Revenantists. They had promised salvation in Sharrow-Met's return, but that had never come. But we, the heralds of a new age, could make it happen, in me."

Shamil righted himself, feeling the many aches that resulted from having been snatched out of the air by a blue falcon. Groaning, he shifted closer to Lyvia, peering intently at her face and seeing it anew. Suddenly, the reasons for her sharp aversion to comparisons with her forebear became plain.

"You were going to pretend to be her," he said. "Sharrow-Met reborn."

"It was Crucio's idea, of course. I would be the vessel for her returned soul, for who would doubt it when a woman wearing this face spoke her words? We would proclaim the Wraith Queen's return and raise the people to tear down the decadent shell that Mara-Vielle had become. But first, some hard measures had to be taken. My face and Sharrow-Met's ancient words would not be enough. The noble houses would not simply stand aside for the new generation, and no coup is ever bloodless."

Her hand moved to the sling on her belt, both fists grasping the narrow leather strap, pulling it taut. "My mother taught me the sling," Lyvia said. "As her mother taught her. The lessons began the day I took my first step and never ended. I barely recall a day I wasn't in my mother's company. I had nurses, tutors, and maids, but Mother was always there, and I never doubted her love. Crucio told me to poison her at dinner the night before our great rebellion. And my father, and my aunt and uncle who were visiting that week. And our chief retainer, for senior servants of the decadent regime could never be trusted. We had a very long list, you see?"

Her hands bunched together, tight enough for the knuckles to turn bone white. "It was the list that stopped me. There were so many names. So many people I knew and loved. I just … couldn't." Her hands relaxed as she let out a long, weary sigh. "So, I took my copy of the list to my mother, who took it to my father. By morning they were building the gallows in the great square.

"Many of my fellow conspirators met their ends with stout hearts and defiant words, but Crucio wasn't brave. All his fine rhetoric, all his apparent wisdom became just sobs and begging as they dragged him to the noose. He was the last to die, and by the time his legs had stopped kicking, I realised I was no longer in love with him, if I ever truly had been. I knew full well the consequences of my act. I knew my own family would condemn me and so was surprised when my turn at the gallows never came. The blood that flows in my veins, Sharrow-Met's blood, was considered too precious to spill, and so I was permitted exile and a chance at redemption."

She turned to Shamil, leaning closer, voice earnest now. "But the notion that redemption can be won here is a lie. Haven't you noticed how many sentinels have their discs, yet they never leave? Because they know this is the only place in all the world they can find a welcome. Because this is where they belong, where I belong. Our sins are too great, our disgrace too deep. But you, Shamil, do not belong here. Whatever you did, or think you did, it should never have brought you to the Eyrie. The greatwings see it, even if you don't."

She put a hand on his neck, drawing him close until their foreheads touched. Shamil was seized by the urge to pull away, spit harsh words at her, but the tremble he felt as their skin met stopped him. "You can climb down from here," she said in a choked whisper before drawing away.

Shamil watched her move stiffly towards Vintress. The bird gulped down a morsel of goat flesh, talons clutching what remained of the carcass as Lyvia climbed onto her back. She afforded Shamil a final glance, mouth opening to voice her farewell, but the words would never be heard.

A sudden thunderous roar from the east drowned all sound, Shamil's gaze snapping to the Maw to see a massive plume of smoke erupting from its depths, driven by a gout of flame. Throughout their time at the Eyrie, the Maw would occasionally belch more smoke than usual, letting out a rumbling groan in the process, but this dwarfed all previous disturbances.

The smoke rose to mountainous heights, roiling black and grey, lightning flashing in its depths as it swirled around Sharrow-Met's statue. Somehow the monument failed to be swallowed by the roiling clouds, rendered instead a pale silhouette. Shamil saw more flashes in the smoke, not lightning this time, brief spherical blossoms of light he was quick to recognise as exploding crystals. The flashes continued for some time until a dark speck appeared, growing into the shape of a fire wing, flying alone and driving hard towards the Eyrie.

"Ashinta and Hareld left on patrol this morning," Lyvia said, exchanging a wide-eyed glance with Shamil.

The fire wing swept overhead as a fresh gout of smoke and flame issued from the Maw, Shamil hearing something in the accompanying roar, something that mixed animalistic rage with deep, ravening hunger. The sense of witnessing a dire awakening was inescapable, Rignar's words sounding loud in Shamil's mind: *As long as there is malice in the world, so will the Voice contrive to persist.*

"Take me with you!" he said, rushing towards Lyvia as Vintress flared her wings. Seeing the indecision on her face, he clasped Lyvia's arm, words flowing from his mouth in a rapid torrent. "You're wrong. I do belong here. I killed a captive. A raptorile snared during a raid into the desert and pushed into the Anverest arena to be slaughtered. It was to be my graduation from the Doctrinate, my confirmation as a warrior in the city guard. And I did it. I fought it, and I killed it. But before the final blow, I looked into its eyes and knew it to be no different from me. It felt. It feared. It *thought*."

His grip tightened on her arm, and Vintress let out a warning hiss as he pressed closer looking for understanding in Lyvia's startled gaze. "They told us they were animals. Beasts who merely mimicked the language and custom they saw in humans. Vermin deserving of only death. It was all a lie. A putrid web of deceit spun so our people could keep raiding their lands and calling ourselves heroes as we plundered and killed. That was my disgrace, Lyvia. My weakness. I saw the lie, and still I killed for it."

He sighed and released her arm, stepping back, forcing himself to meet her eye despite his shame. "I belong here as much as you do," he told her, making no effort to conceal the desperate plea in his voice. "Please. Take me with you."

• ♦ •

THE EYRIE WAS ALL BUSTLE AND PREPARATION WHEN Vintress landed on one of the outer rises, releasing Shamil from the ungentle cage of her talons to suffer a hard landing on the tiered steps. Lyvia climbed down from the falcon's back, and they both went in search of Tihla, dodging around sentinels laden with bundled arrows and sundry weapons. Their questions were swallowed by the plethora of orders echoing about the place, Morgath's voice loudest among them, itself occasionally drowned out by the squawks and screeches of the many greatwings alighting on the tall perches. Despite the general din, Shamil caught a few of Morgath's commands, "... form two companies ... falcons go high, fire wings go low, owls will guard the rear and the flanks ..."

Shamil managed to snare Ehlias's arm as he made for the central rise with a brace of claw spears, the smith pointing him towards Rignar's chamber in response to his shouted question.

"What's happening?" Shamil pressed.

Ehlias spared only a grim-eyed glance and a grunted reply before hurrying on his way. "Battle, lad. What else?"

They found Tihla watching Rignar tend to a trio of deep cuts in Ashinta's shoulder. The mage held a piece of carnelian in one hand and jasper in the other, both stones glowing bright as he held them close to the wounds. The cuts were closing, albeit slowly, the healing causing Ashinta a considerable amount of pain judging by the answers she hissed through clenched teeth in response to Tihla's barrage of questions.

"Told you ..." She gave a hard grunt, eyes closing tight for a moment as Rignar completed sealing one of her scars. "Never seen one like that before. Thought it might be some kind of bat at first ..." She broke off, biting down a yell before mastering herself. "But its wings sprouted from its back. Had a body like a man, covered in fur and shorter overall but longer of limb." She let out a grating laugh, casting a rueful glance at her partly healed shoulder. "With sharp claws, but still, mostly manlike.

And its eyes …" She shuddered, this time not due to the pain of her injuries. "Big as apples and black like jet. Saw the hate in them plain enough, though."

Ashinta hissed and shot Rignar a reproachful look as the second scar sealed shut before switching her gaze back to Tihla. "And they're fast, falcon speed. They were on me and Hareld before we knew it, streaking out of the smoke from all directions. Him and his bird were already falling by the time I knew what was happening."

"So," Rignar said, raising his brows, though his eyes remained focused on his work. "The Maw has coughed out some new horrors, it seems."

"It's not just the man-bats, mage. Like I told the First Wing, there were plenty of flensers and scythers about too, not to mention what was happening on the ground. Couldn't see much with all the smoke, but there were vehlgard marching out of the Maw in columns, several thousand of the cack-eaters. Looked like they were taking a westward course."

"That would lead them straight into the lava flow," Tihla said. Shamil saw the tension in her bearing, well controlled though it was, betrayed most clearly in the single vein pulsing in her temple.

"Just saying what I saw." Ashinta's face bunched, nostrils flaring and skin reddening as Rignar closed the last cut.

"Your bird?" Tihla asked her.

"Few tail feathers lost is all." Ashinta reached for her helm and hopped down from Rignar's bench. "We can still fly."

"Good. Load up on arrows and make ready. You'll wing with me when we launch." Tihla's gaze shifted to Lyvia, as if noting her presence for the first time. "You too. Fill your pouches with crystal and get aloft. Lamira has charge of the falcon wing. Stay close and follow her lead. I've no time for any more lessons, and we need every bird in the air."

Lyvia shared a brief but bright glance with Shamil, lips wavering as she sought words that wouldn't come until he gave her a tight smile and nodded. Scooping a handful of quartz into a leather pouch, she rushed off into the shouts and squawks outside.

"I've a notion we'll soon have need of more stones," Tihla said to Rignar, who was already setting out a row of crystals on his bench.

"I'll see to it," he said, looking up at Shamil. "I'd work faster knowing there was someone here to watch my back."

Tihla's gaze slid to Shamil, evident reluctance in her eyes. "We've no true picture of what we face today. The Eyrie may be swarmed by all manner of Maw-born foulness before this is over, and you have no obligation here now …"

"Yes," he cut in. "I do."

The Second Wing sighed and inclined her head in acquiescence. "As you wish. Fetch your weapons and guard the mage. If none of us return by sunset, climb down and get as far west as you can, spread the word that the Voice has woken."

She went to a corner where a claw spear had been propped, augmented by several fragments of topaz set into the sickle-shaped blade. "Thanks for this," she told Rignar over her shoulder. "Let's hope it works."

◆ ◆ ◆

HE WATCHED VINTRESS CARRY LYVIA ALOFT TO JOIN THE circling flock of falcons. Tihla took off soon after on Rhienvelk, a veteran fire wing with a cracked beak and plumage a dark shade of crimson. The sentinels formed into three spirals in accordance with the First Wing's orders, the fire wings being the largest and spread out over a half mile or more of sky.

Morgath Durnholm was the last to fly off, climbing onto Fleyrak's back to pause for a momentary survey of the mostly empty Eyrie. His face was hidden by his helm, but Shamil had the sense of a man saying farewell to a much-loved home. The blank glass eyes of Morgath's visor settled on Shamil, lowered once in a bow of grave respect, then jerked upwards as the First Wing gave a voiceless command that had Fleyrak leaping from the perch. The bird's wings sent twin whirlwinds spinning across the Eyrie as he climbed into the sky, immediately striking out towards the Maw.

As the First Wing passed below, the three circles broke apart to follow, the falcons staying high, whilst the fire wings fell in behind Morgath, spreading out into a formation that resembled a broad arrowhead. The owls were the smallest contingent and flew a good distance behind the fire wings, their formation more varied in height so that, as they drew away, they resembled a giant shield.

Shamil paced continuously as he watched the winged host fade towards the ever more mountainous smoke. He had primed his bow with a quartz-head arrow and half drawn the string, mainly to occupy his hands as seething frustration rose to an ever greater pitch.

Besides him and Rignar, the only other occupants of the Eyrie were Kritzlasch, circling above, and Ehlias. The smith sat outside the door to his workshop cradling a windlass crossbow, his song a murmured dirge now, full of dire intonations. The crossbow was loaded with a bolt armed with a chunk of white quartz the size of a fist. Four other identical devices, all drawn

and loaded, were propped against the wall within easy reach.

Ehlias's song fell silent as Shamil paced closer, his restive gaze roaming the arrayed weapons. "Too heavy to aim from a bird's back," the smith explained, patting the crossbow's stock. "Made 'em when I first came here and didn't know any better. Kept them out of sentiment, I s'pose." He gave a wry, strained chuckle. "Never thought I'd have occasion to use 'em, to be honest. Still, reckon I'll get at least a hundred or so beasties before they gobble me up."

His words were drowned by a loud rumble of thunder from the Maw. Shamil's head snapped round to see the last dark specks of the sentinel host disappearing into the smoke. The flash and glimmer of exploding crystals began almost immediately, made even more disconcerting because the sounds of battle took several seconds to reach the Eyrie.

"I'd give just about anything to be there out with them," Ehlias said. "Guess you would too. Not an easy thing to be a sentinel without a bird. I had one, y'know. Rhottblane, means 'red snow' in my birth tongue. He was an owl, pure white all over but for his eyes, red like rubies. It was age rather than battle that got him in the end. Couldn't hunt, couldn't see much of anything, shedding feathers that wouldn't grow back. One day, he just flew off, never saw him again. I tried to bond with another, but no bird would do more than snatch meat from me. Even thought about trying my luck with him once." Ehlias jerked his head at the summit of the nest. "Turned out, I was too much of a coward when the time came."

Following his gaze, Shamil saw a very large winged shape circling the nest, black but for the speckle of sunlight on its feathers. "Stielbek," he murmured. He found his gaze captured by the black wing's slowly turning silhouette, a singular irresistible notion building in his mind that caused him to return the arrow to his quiver and hook his bow over his chest.

"Yes," Ehlias mused, puzzlement colouring his tone. "Odd he should turn up again now. Usually only appears when there's a new brace of fledglings …"

Ehlias's voice faltered as Shamil started off at a run, buckling his helm in place, which had the fortuitous effect of muffling the baffled words the smith cast in his wake. "What're you about, lad?"

Shamil sprinted through the Eyrie, skirting the rises and making for the cliff where the beam pointed towards the smoke now lit by so much unleashed sorcery its upper reaches had taken on a persistent shimmer. Shamil didn't pause upon reaching the beam, didn't even look up before he came to the end and leapt. As his feet left the timber, part of him knew this to be madness, that when he fell this time, there would be no one to save him. He was just a lost youth with a broken mind hurtling towards his own death because he feared the guilt and self-detestation that was his due. Still he refused to surrender to despair, letting the hope blossom like a fire as he reached the apex of his leap, allowing only one clear thought to rise to the forefront of his churning mind: *He was waiting for me … for me to be ready. He was waiting for me …*

Stielbek caught him before he had even begun to fall.

NINE

The Maw

STIELBEK'S TALONS CLASPED HIM ONLY FOR A
second before tossing him into the air. The momentary
terror gave rise to a notion that the bird had allowed him
to experience the joy of salvation only to let him fall, a cruel
amusement born of his avian mind. However, a gust of wind
and a brush of feathers saw him land on the black wing's back.
His legs quickly found purchase on the hard, surging muscle
beneath the plumage at the nape of Stielbek's neck. Shamil secured himself in place by clutching fistfuls of feathers for want
of a harness. Stielbek angled his huge head to regard him with
a gleaming yellow eye, and it was then that Shamil felt the bond
for the first time.

He found the sensation to resemble the satisfaction that
came from sinking an arrow into the centre of a target, or the
turn of a key in a lock, but greatly magnified. It was a feeling
of completion, of two matched components fitting together.
Suddenly, Shamil understood the nature of the bond between
sentinel and bird. It was not a sharing of minds, but a sharing
of purpose. Staring into the depths of Stielbek's eye, Shamil
felt himself dwarfed by the intense commitment he saw there,
the absolute conviction in the soul behind those eyes. He found
himself lost in the utter blackness of the pupil, experiencing a
sense of being drawn into depthless shadows where there lurked
many ugly things. Bonding with this mighty and ancient soul
was like being scraped by a gnarled tree, one that cared little for
what such scraping might do to its rider.

Apparently satisfied, Stielbek's eye flashed white as he blinked before turning his head towards the Maw, sail-sized wings
rising and falling in mighty sweeps that took them high into
the sky. The black wing levelled out at a height that put them
several hundred feet above the Maw, and Shamil's nostrils suffered a sulphurous sting as they drew ever nearer. The struggle
within the vast column of smoke seemed to be continuing with
unabated fury, but now he caught glimpses of the combatants.

Birds wheeled and dove, fleeting spectres against the pulsing
glow of detonating crystals. Smaller shadows flickered amongst
them, dark irregular shapes that swarmed and broke apart amidst
blossoms of white light. As Stielbek flew closer, the glare of
magical luminescence became so bright Shamil was forced to
snick the lever on the side of his helm, slotting the dark glass in
place. The view immediately shifted from occluded confusion to
chaotic and terrible clarity, the impenetrable smoke rendered a

vague greyish mist.

He saw a bird mobbed by winged creatures the size of cats, presumably flensers. The dense mass of them heaved like bees around a hive as they overwhelmed the bird, and Shamil found it impossible to discern the identity of the rider amongst the flurry of leathery wings and gnashing teeth. The greatwing thrashed and twisted, shedding feathers and slain enemies, but it was clear this contest would only end one way.

The uneven struggle continued as Stielbek swept closer. Shamil unslung his bow and reached for an arrow, but before he could take aim, the struggling bird and its assailants disappeared in a blossom of fire as the unseen rider found a way to detonate one of their crystals. The debris slipped away beneath them, Stielbek broadening his wings to glide through a dwindling cloud of feathers. A few flensers, having survived the blast, sought to bar their path, and Shamil heard their hungry, yipping shrieks even above the rushing wind.

Drawing his bow, he let fly at the lead creature, the crystal-head striking it in the chest and blowing it apart along with two of its companions. Only one remained, streaking towards them undaunted, its cries rising to deafening volume as it closed. Seeing its face clearly, Shamil found himself confronted by a ravening mask of teeth, its snapping jaws adding a ululation to its unending scream. But it was the hate in its eyes that snared Shamil's attention, causing him to freeze in the act of reaching for another arrow. Black orbs shot through with veins of red that coalesced to form a blazing pupil, they glowed with vicious, insatiable hunger beyond even the most starved lion or desert wolf. As it loomed before him, jaws snapping so fast its teeth blurred, Shamil had no doubt this was a creature bred purely for the purpose of wreaking the ugliest death on any human unfortunate enough to encounter it.

Stielbek raised his head in an almost casual gesture, beak opening and closing with a hard snap. The flenser vanished, the only trace of its passing a vaporous spatter on Shamil's visor. The increased sting to his nostrils and ashen catch in his throat made it clear that they were now in the heart of the smokestack, the air rent by repeated percussive blasts and screams he hoped came only from the throats of the Maw's creations.

Stielbek turned as Shamil caught sight of another bird below, an owl, the sentinel on its back turning loose arrows at the flensers swarming in pursuit. Shamil put a pair of his own crystal-heads into their midst and was rewarded with the sight of two satisfyingly large explosions before Stielbek folded his wings, sending them into a near vertical dive straight into th heart of the swarm.

For an instant the world became a fury of choked-off screa and the crack of sundered bones and skulls, and Shamil fel increasing wetness where his skin was exposed to the air. He c only hold on as the black wing twisted and spun, thighs cla hard to the heaving muscle and one hand gripping feather white knuckles as the other strove to keep hold of his b

Then they were through, Stielbek assuming a leve that enabled Shamil to wipe the red slick from his visor. around he saw they were alone once again, surrounde drifting vapour through which occasional patches o gleamed harsh through his darkened lenses.

A laugh came unbidden from Shamil's throat, d joy but an uncomfortable concordance of relief and As Stielbek banked and took them lower, Shamil r glimpse of a greatwing during the climb to the Eyrie, his hunger to know what it might feel like to traverse the skies with such a beast. The reality, it transpired, was everything he had hoped for, despite the horrors witnessed and the certainty of more to come, and so he laughed, long and loud.

The attack came without warning, a hard stunning impact to the top of his helm that would surely have shattered his skull but for its protection. He reeled, legs slackening and losing purchase on Stielbek's neck. He would have fallen if the black wing hadn't abruptly angled his body, jolting Shamil back to awareness. Blinking, he shook away the haze that marred his vision, wincing at the sharp pain in his head and flexing his left hand in angry realisation that he had lost his bow.

A loud, guttural cry from behind caused Shamil to turn, seeing a broad-winged shape labouring in the disturbed air left in Stielbek's wake. It was two-thirds the size of a blue falcon, but any similarity ended there. This bird was dark grey in colour, its featherless neck long and coiling like a snake, emitting the same throaty call all the while. It had a wickedly sharp beak shaped like a butcher's hook, but Shamil saw more danger in its talons, far larger in proportion to the bird's body than could be natural, each one a long black sickle.

"Scyther," Shamil grunted. The reason for the beast's repeated calls became clear when three more swept out of the mist to fly alongside it. He began to reach for his whip but was forced to grab a fistful of feathers when Stielbek went into a sudden dive. Shamil glimpsed the sight of another, far larger, bird just ahead. Something flicked the air just above his helm, and the now familiar blast of exploding quartz sounded to the rear.

Recognition dawned as the approaching bird swept overhead, and Shamil noted how the dark glass of his visor rendered Vintress's feathers a verdant shade of green rather than blue. He saw Lyvia whirl her sling and cast another missile at a scyther as it banked towards her, transforming it into a ball of grey mist in a flash of combusting crystal. Stielbek shortened his wings and pivoted, raising his talons to rend the two surviving Maw beasts apart as they closed. The grisly task complete, he spread his wings into a broad arc, catching an updraft that enabled him to hover.

Vintress circled them in a tight arc, and Shamil noted the blackened and scorched feathers on the falcon's breast, though he heaved a relieved sigh at seeing her rider uninjured. He stared hard at the blank eyes of Lyvia's visor, hoping there was a welcoming smile behind it. She stared back for a second, then pointed, her finger stabbing downwards towards the orange-red snake of the lava flow. Black shapes flicked and spiralled across it, sentinels and swarms of Maw beasts engaged in a deadly dance. Through the chaos of battle his gaze caught something more, a flurry of pale white specks at the flow's edge that put him in mind of a snowstorm, surely something that couldn't be possible.

Sensing his curiosity, Stielbek drew his wings back to send them into a dive with Vintress following close on their tail. They streaked down through a dozen swirling duels, Shamil blinking his eyes against the repeated flare of discharged sorcery whilst the hellish cacophony of rage and pain penetrated his helm with irksome ease. He could feel the heat of the lava now, building in intensity as they swept lower and beading his skin with sweat. A small, somewhat bedraggled swarm of flensers tried to bar their path, many leaking blood from recent wounds, their wings pierced or torn in places, causing Shamil to wonder how they still manage managed to fly. He sensed Stielbek's disdain as he continued to dive, not troubling himself to change course and cutting his way through the beasts with a few well-placed snaps of his beak before levelling out some three hundred feet from the surface of the molten river.

The sounds of conflict faded as they glided across the steaming, bubbling surface, and Shamil's nose and mouth flooded in response to the foul gasses. He could see the far bank of the flow through the shimmering curtain of heated air. Blinking tears to clear his vision, Shamil was shocked to find himself confronted by an army, tall spears rising like a vast forest from dark ranks. The distance was still too great to make out their features, but he knew these must be the dreaded vehlgard, the two-legged fodder of the Voice's malign horde said to be the obscene result of some unnatural fusion of man and beast. They were arrayed in neat, unmoving columns from the lip of the Maw to the edge of the glowing river, a thick black line thousands strong broken in the centre by the blaze of white Shamil had seen from above.

As Stielbek took him closer, he saw to his amazement that his first thought had been correct; this was a snowstorm. Or rather, he realised as the near overpowering heat gave way to a sudden chill and a lacelike veil began to cover his visor, an ice storm. As frost clustered on his brow, Stielbek let out a brief, throaty cry of protest and beat his wings to take them higher. Shamil leaned forward to stare down into the heart of the raging storm below, seeing great plumes of rising steam as lava met ice and turned instantly to rock. Upon nearing the slope leading to the lip of the Maw, the wall of white suddenly diminished, revealing the eastern bank in full.

Although the air remained thick with mingled steam and smoke, Shamil managed to make out a dozen dark figures below. They stood in a line close to the storm, each one holding aloft a staff, tips blazing with the unmistakable glow unique to crystalmancy. Streams of pale blue energy emerged continually from the twelve staffs, curving in chaotic spirals before merging with the raging chaos of the ice storm.

"Mages," Shamil realised in a whisper. "The Voice has mages of its own."

As if hearing his words, all dozen figures instantly turned their eyes skyward. Their faces were indistinct, but he saw that they were all clad in mismatched clothing, long trailing silks contrasting with archaic armour or cloaks of fur. However, their disparity in appearance was dispelled by the uniform glow of the eyes they focused on Shamil, as fiery red and full of hateful hunger as the flenser Stielbek had dispatched only moments before.

It was then that Stielbek gave full vent to his cry. Shamil had heard little of his voice so far and found the volume of it enough to shake his very bones. It bore little relation to the high-pitched screech of a fire wing or falcon, pitched lower even than an owl's hoots. It was more of a roar, full of rage and a depth of enmity Shamil could feel through the bond along with a deeper understanding; Stielbek knew these mages of old and wanted very badly to kill them.

The mages lowered their staffs as Stielbek's cry faded, the arcing streams of energy blinking out as they raised their red eyes to regard the black wing. It may have been something conjured by his overburdened mind, but Shamil was sure their eyes all blazed brighter in that moment, though he saw no change in their stance or expression. However, the sense of hatred being returned in full measure was palpable.

One of the mages in particular caught his eye, a tall, bare-chested man of impressive stature. Shamil quickly flipped the lever on his helm, switching to the magnifying lenses to gain a better view, finding himself confronted with an angular, hollow-cheeked face, the man's well-muscled frame and bald head covered all over in a dense matrix of tattoos. Shamil once again wondered if his sight were playing him true, for the tattoos seemed to be moving, coiling and overlapping like snakes trapped within his skin. As if in response to the scrutiny, the tattooed man blinked his red eyes and angled his head. Shamil caught the unmistakable curve of a smile to his lips before Stielbek abruptly turned away and the view was lost.

Facing to the front, Shamil switched his visor back to the standard lenses in time to see an inverted rain of fire filling the sky directly ahead. Stielbek swept his wings in rapid beats, sending them higher. Shamil ducked as something fast and flaming streaked within a foot of his helm, half-a-dozen more trailing smoke as they whooshed past. Glancing up at the sound of a pealing cry, he saw Vintress rapidly disappearing into the pall above, rider and bird swallowed by the smoke before any fire arrows could claim them.

Hearing a loud hiss of annoyance, Shamil looked down to find an arrow had left a patch of burning embers on Stielbek's wingtip. He watched with relief as it dwindled to a blackened stain before it could birth a blaze. The origin of this fiery barrage became obvious when Stielbek went into a steep bank. Fire arrows blazed along the leading edges of the vehlgard columns as archers raised their bows and loosed concentrated volleys. Luckily, they were now too high for the arrows to reach them, though Shamil saw one sentinel who wasn't so lucky.

The fire wing swerved through the air in an effort to dodge

the blizzard of fiery shafts, but the smoke trailing from twin blazes in each wing told of a grim and inevitable fate. In addition to the countless arrows seeking to bring it down, it was being pursued by three Maw beasts Shamil hadn't yet encountered but was quick to identify.

"Man-bats!" he hissed, matching Ashinta's description to the human-sized creatures with huge black eyes and leathery wings that sprouted from their backs. Two were armed with what appeared to be ten-foot-long tridents, but the one in the lead carried some form of overlarge crossbow.

Shamil watched in growing dismay as the man-bat raised the weapon and triggered the lock. The melon-sized projectile ignited soon after being launched, bursting into a sparking ball of blazing light. It described an elegant arc through the air to impact on the fire wing's tail, bursting apart with a flurry of shimmering particles that Shamil might have found pretty at another time. His dismay turned to outright horror as the fire wing transformed into an ugly ball of broken wings and trailing feathers, and the identity of its rider became clear.

Morgath Durnholm held on to his bird's harness for only a few seconds before his muscular form was cast away, bird and rider tumbling towards the army below with the man-bats screaming triumph and diving in pursuit. Shamil's alarm was enough to send Stielbek into a steep descent, the black wing beating his wings to produce a daunting turn of speed. One man-bat noticed their approach and immediately abandoned its dive to place itself in their path, swinging its long trident around in a slash at Stielbek's head as they closed. Shamil flicked his wrist, and the raptorile-tail whip uncoiled with blurring speed, the topaz tip entwining the three spikes of the man-bat's trident before discharging its sorcerous energy. Lightning danced along the spear's length then up the arms of its wielder, transforming both into a blackened and twisted mess that tumbled away as Shamil jerked the whip free.

Stielbek streaked between the two remaining man-bats, killing one with his beak and the other, his claws. Spreading his wings wide and rearing back, the black wing extended his talons to enfold the tumbling form of Morgath Durnholm. They were barely fifty feet from the ground now, the air a maelstrom of fire arrows that would surely see them ablaze within seconds.

A chorus of bird cries drew Shamil's gaze upwards in time to see what appeared to be the entire Sentinel host streaking out of the sky. Tihla flew at their head with Lyvia close behind, sling whirling. Crystal-headed arrows fell in a thick hail, the neat ranks of the vehlgard column below blasted apart by a welter of explosions.

Stielbek was forced to swoop low before soaring high, and Shamil found himself staring down into the face of a vehlgard barely a spear's length beneath. Having expected to be confronted with some form of bestial, snarling mask, he was surprised to see a face that was recognisably human in both expression and form. The features were certainly broader than could be called natural, with a blocklike jaw and wide lips, the pale, hairless skin scarred in many places and rich in tattoos of garish design. But still he saw humanity in the way he glared at Shamil, lips drawn back from wedge-like teeth in a snarl of anger. This was not the unreasoning, animalistic hunger of the Maw beasts. These were the eyes of a thinking being like the raptorile he had murdered. But unlike the raptorile, the soul behind these eyes badly wanted him dead.

The vehlgard lunged at him just as Stielbek beat his wings to begin his ascent, and Shamil heard a shout of frustrated rage as the long spear flailed at the black wing's tail feathers. A deep, growling voice chased them with curses in a grating language alien to Shamil's ear, fading quickly.

The sentinels closed in around Stielbek as he climbed into the upper reaches of the still roiling smokestack, soaring clear of arrow range but soon finding themselves attacked by a fresh swarm of flensers. Tihla was quick to hurl her fire wing into the heart of the swarm, the crystals set into her claw spear shining bright as she whirled it. Sparks erupted whenever it met the flesh of a Maw beast, sending a dozen blackened corpses towards the ground. Shamil lashed his whip constantly as Stielbek took them through the fray, the swarm soon blasted apart as the sentinels exhausted their remaining crystals, and they finally flew clear of the smoke.

Tihla's bird laboured to the front of the formation, the Second Wing waving her spear in a slow circle before pointing it at the Eyrie. They were being ordered home. Surveying the surviving host, Shamil saw the reason in stark clarity. Less than half were left, and many of those were either injured or close to exhaustion. Riders sagged on the backs of their birds, several clutching wounds. Many of the greatwings were also in poor shape, leaving a trail of dark specks in their wake as they shed feathers, some bearing blackened patches on their plumage, others leaking crimson droplets as they struggled towards the Eyrie on tired wings. The Sentinels had suffered a defeat this day, and the unmoving form of the man lying limp in Stielbek's claws made it clear they might be about to suffer their most grievous loss yet.

The Mage's Gambit

RIGNAR LABOURED THROUGH THE NIGHT, TIHLA lingering outside his chamber as the glimmer of powerful sorcery flickered in the edges of the closed door. An occasional shout would accompany the shifting lights, weak at first but growing in volume as the hours wore on. Shamil wasn't sure whether this was a good sign or not.

By unanimous agreement, the other sentinels had all refused to accept crystal healing to allow Rignar to concentrate his entire energies on the First Wing. Consequently, Shamil had spent much of the night employing the medical skills he had learned in the Doctrinate. It amounted mostly to setting broken bones and stitching cuts, some small, others deep. However, much of the burden of caring for the wounded fell on Ehlias. The smith possessed many years of hard-won experience in tending injury, although his remedies ranged from the basic to the gruesome, the latter involving some judicious use of red-hot irons or the sharper knives from his workshop. Liberal quantities of pain-muting herbs were also doled out, resulting in a curiously lighthearted atmosphere amongst the wounded. Songs and jokes filled the air, although Shamil noted that the laughter had a near hysterical quality, often subsiding to tears in quieter moments as confusion was replaced by the hard realisation of grief.

The greatwings settled on their perches or returned to the nest, some keening laments for lost riders, others nuzzling beaks at wounded comrades. Shamil noted that Stielbek kept apart from them, perching on a rise close to the eastern cliff from where he maintained an unwavering vigil of the Maw. Its roar was louder now, hunger and rage more discernible than ever, leaving Shamil in no doubt that he was hearing the Voice itself. The legends had always depicted this eternal adversary as more a malign seducer than a monster, whispering temptation into the ears of weak or greedy souls. The sound that now emerged from the Maw spoke of something different, a being perhaps transformed by its centuries of confinement. This altered Voice, Shamil knew, had no interest in the subtleties of seduction or carefully woven schemes; it hungered only for the destruction of those that had chained it.

After he had stitched his last cut and wiped his last fevered brow, Shamil climbed the rise to stand at Stielbek's side. Even without the insight offered by their bond, he could sense the black wing's roiling fury, the deep desire for a return to battle in the eyes he focused on the shifting glow of the Maw.

"The mage with the tattoos," Shamil said. "An old friend, perhaps?"

Stielbek cocked his head slightly, beak snapping once in confirmation. "Who is he, I wonder?" Shamil peered at the ugly spectacle of the Maw at night. Sharrow-Met's statue stood silhouetted against the constant smoke lit in various hues by the glow of lava and the mage's magics, which had continued unabated since the sentinels' retreat.

The ice storm they crafted was invisible in the dark, but its effects were now increasingly evident. A black line had appeared in the slow current of the molten river, a line pointing west that hadn't been there the night before. It seemed barely more than a hair's width at this distance, but Shamil calculated it must be at least fifty feet across.

"So," he murmured. "That's what they're about."

Stielbek's beak snapped again, louder this time. His desire for resumed battle was clear, but the bond enabled Shamil to sense something beneath it, a raw impatience to finish this task so that they might begin another.

"Soon." Shamil ran a hand through the feathers on Stielbek's neck before turning to descend the rise, making quickly for Rignar's chamber.

◆ ◆ ◆

"THEY'RE CRAFTING A BRIDGE."

Morgath spared Shamil a brief glance, grunting as he swung his legs off Rignar's bed. The mage had sealed the First Wing's every wound, but his broad back was now an epic of overlapping scars, and crystalmancy could do nothing to restore the eye he had lost. In its place he wore a smooth blue stone, veined in gold, a strangely beautiful island of colour in a sea of scarred flesh. More concerning than the disfigurement was the absence of any vestige of a smile on his lips. Shamil had thought this man capable of finding humour in any circumstance, and discovering his error made for a harsh realisation: *he thinks we've already lost.*

"He's right," Tihla put in. "Took a look for myself. That ice storm they've conjured can turn twenty yards of lava to rock in the space of an hour. By noon tomorrow they'll have a causeway for that army to cross."

"Only if they have mages to keep the storm churning," Shamil said. "We need to kill them."

"Mind your place." Tihla's voice was curt, though less so than he might have expected. "What you did today was impressive, and we're all rightly grateful for it, but the First Wing decides our battle plans, not you. Today we lost half our number and barely got within sight of those mages. And even if we did get close enough for an arrow, I doubt they'll just stand there and obligingly await death." She took a breath heavy with reluctance. "It might be wiser to conserve our strength, wait for them to cross before launching successive attacks, buy time for the Treaty Realms to gather their forces."

She fell silent, eyes lingering expectantly on Morgath's slumped head, her features bunching in suppressed consternation when no response was immediately forthcoming.

"Shamil is right."

Shamil and Tihla turned to regard Rignar as he hefted his satchel onto his bench. "It will take weeks for Mara-Vielle and the Crucible Kingdom to muster an army," he went on. "Months for the Treaty Realms entire to gather a force capable of defeating the malign horde, if such a force can even be gathered. We have to stop this before it begins."

"You want me to watch the rest of them die?"

Morgath's voice was a raw scraping echo of its previous vitality. Looking into his partly ruined face with its gleaming blue eye, Shamil knew his wounds went deeper than mere skin and muscle. The First Wing of the Sentinel Eyrie might not yet be broken, but he was at least buckled.

"This family we've built?" Morgath continued, his gaze shifting from Rignar to Tihla. "I did that once before. All my fine lads and lasses, thieves and cutthroats they may have been, but they were family to me. I knew more loyalty and kindness living amongst pirates than I ever knew throughout the long, wretched years beneath my father's roof. And I watched him hang them all, one by one. He had me chained in such a way that I couldn't turn my head from the sight, and I was flogged if I dared to close my eyes. When I was dragged to these mountains and dumped at the base of the Eyrie, the last words I ever heard from my father were, 'Die quickly.' But I wouldn't, my last act of defiance. In surviving here, I won the trust of my brothers and sisters, once again becoming a captain of sorts. In the years since, the love I have for this place and these people has washed away all the anger and hatred that once claimed my soul. Don't ask me to destroy what's left, Tihla." His head slumped once more, ragged voice descending into a groan. "I can't."

"You won't have to," Rignar said. He paused to undo the satchel's buckles, revealing the glassy orb of the black onyx. "If I might be so bold as to propose a stratagem."

· ♦ ·

"IT DOESN'T SEEM LIKE NEARLY ENOUGH."

Morgath's one good eye tracked over the three birds perched on the east-facing rise. Kritzlasch and Vintress exchanged a few beak snaps and hisses as they waited, both resting on a branch lower than Stielbek and conscientious in avoiding his eye. For his part, the black wing seemed content to ignore them both, his gaze still entirely locked on the Maw and its vomitous smoke. The rising sun painted the occluded horizon a faint shade of pink. Deep shadows still concealed much of the army waiting on the far bank of the lava flow, but the ice storm was visible now, a blaze of white that seemed to be growing by the second.

"Speed is more important than numbers," Rignar replied, glancing up from the black onyx. He had kept hold of the crystal since Morgath's eventual and grudging agreement to this plan, constantly playing his fingers over the surface. The stone's response to his touch had grown ever brighter in the intervening hours, producing a sustained shimmer in its core. Judging by Rignar's increasingly grey and hollow-cheeked countenance, Shamil concluded that whatever sorcery he had crafted within its facets had cost him dear.

"Besides"—Rignar forced a smile before favouring Lyvia and Shamil with a fond glance—"I'd rather fly with my young friends at my side than any other."

Morgath gave a sombre nod before settling his gaze first on Shamil then Lyvia. "I won't command you to this," he told them, the diminished rasp of his voice battling with the stiff morning wind. "No disgrace will result if you choose not to ..."

"We're wasting time," Lyvia cut in, before adding with a tight smile, "But your consideration is appreciated, First Wing."

Morgath's livid scars twisted as a very faint grin ghosted across his face, but only briefly before he turned and strode away. He climbed the perch of the tallest rise where Kaitlahr waited. The youthful fire wing had taken up station at the beam before sunrise, crouching low to allow the First Wing to climb onto his back with no need to leap. Other greatwings had issued forth from the nest to accept sentinels whose birds had succumbed to their wounds. Even so, the host mustered that morning was a much denuded and less impressive gathering than had flown to confront the resurgent Voice the day before.

Before the sentinels buckled on their helms, Shamil saw a mostly uniform expression of fatalistic determination with no sign of the usual grim humour. He watched Morgath share a long look with Tihla before they both donned their helms, a look that surely spoke of many things left unsaid throughout the years of their service.

They took off in one great flock, the well-ordered grouping of yesterday replaced by a dense arrowhead formation aimed directly at the Maw. The air thrummed as the birds beat their wings with furious energy, closing the distance to their foes with a speed that commanded notice.

Rignar waited until the sentinels closed to within a few hundred yards of the Maw before donning his helm. "It's time," he said, raising his gaze to Kritzlasch, who immediately hopped down from the perch, crouching low so the mage could climb onto his back.

"Before we set off," he said, settling himself into place, one hand clutching the owl's harness and the other pressing the onyx hard against his chest. "It would be remiss of me not to offer my regrets to Lady Lyvia."

"Regrets?" she asked, voice given a metallic tinge by her own helm as she climbed onto Vintress's back.

"For the desecration we are about to inflict upon your ancestor." Rignar nodded to Sharrow-Met's statue, still contriving to shrug off the concealing cloak of the Maw's discharge.

Lyvia replied with a short, tinny laugh. "Desecrate away, good sir. It'll be a relief not to have to look at that thing every day."

Stielbek shuddered with anticipation when Shamil mounted him, spreading his wings and launching them into the air without pause. He climbed into the air to catch an updraft and began to circle higher, letting out an impatient caw that had Vintress and Kritzlasch quickly following suit.

The three birds levelled out at least two hundred feet higher than the sentinel host before striking for the Maw. Shamil could see the close-packed formation of greatwings closing on the smokestack now and the flecks of black within the haze that told of a great many Maw beasts rising to meet their onslaught. Flares of light erupted at the edge of the smoke as the leading sentinels let loose with their first volley of crystal-head arrows before they disappeared into the grey-black fog.

For a few seconds, unleashed energy roiled like a compressed lightning storm, a testament to the ferocity of the hidden struggle, flashing so bright Shamil was forced to switch to his darkened lenses. He fought down a panicked suspicion that the sentinels had met with disaster, and a relieved sigh hissed through his teeth when he saw the leading birds sweep clear of the smoke, followed by what appeared to be most of the host. The sentinels banked upon reaching clear sky, turning in a wide arc to attack once again, loosing a flurry of arrows as they did so. The host became a great wheeling circle at the edge of the towering pall, which darkened in its upper reaches as ever more Maw beasts were drawn towards the fray.

"It's working," Shamil muttered, feeling a thrum of satisfaction from Stielbek. He took them higher still, hopefully beyond

the notice of any enemies, although Shamil wasn't so naive as to think this mission would end without combat. Soon, the now familiar sting of airborne ash reached his nose, and he looked down to see the great monument passing almost directly below. Looking to his left and right he saw Vintress and Kritzlasch flying alongside and raised his hand, forming a fist in a prearranged signal, which they both answered in kind. In accordance with the plan, Lyvia would dive first in the hope that her swift-moving falcon would draw away any Maw beasts lingering in the cloud below. Shamil would follow with Rignar close behind, Stielbek carving a path through any opposition to reach their target.

Shamil shifted his hand to grip the whip's handle. He had secured himself a bow and quiver full of crystal-heads from Ehlias's stores but knew trying to aim and loose during a dive so steep and fast would be next to impossible. The black wing's beak and talons would be their principal weapons today.

Vintress gave a loud screech as she folded her wings and plummeted into the drifted grey-black haze, with Lyvia's sling trailing from her hand as they disappeared from sight. Shamil forced himself to wait the agreed-upon count of five very long seconds before sinking lower, Stielbek's neck feathers fluttering against his visor as he drew in his wings, turned onto his side, and hurtled into the smoke, his course as straight and vertical as any plumb line.

As they fell into the shifting, acrid gloom, Shamil glanced back to confirm Kritzlasch was only a few yards behind before turning to peer into the onrushing sleet of embers and soot. His hand ached as he gripped the whip, and he expected some screaming, hellish visage to loom out of the chaos at any second, but their dive proved uninterrupted. Within the space of no more than five heartbeats, the smoke dissipated to reveal Sharrow-Met's vast, stone features, still somehow beautiful despite their monolithic proportions.

Stielbek voiced a loud screech upon seeing the Wraith Queen's face, and Shamil could hear the clear note of plaintive longing it held. The bird flared his wings as they drew level with the statue's head, banking hard to circle the monument in a downward spiral. Shamil risked another backward glance, finding Rignar had raised himself up on the owl's back, the shining orb of the onyx clutched against his chest. Shamil knew that for this to work, the mage's throw would need to be strong and true, and for all his virtues, the man was no warrior. However, he had insisted that only he could cast the onyx and gave cheery assurances that he hadn't yet failed to place a crystal where it needed to be and wasn't about to start.

The lightning bolt lanced upwards just as Shamil began to turn away, striking Kritzlasch full in the chest and birthing an instant flower of black and red. The bird's wings flailed as he tumbled end over end, casting Rignar from his back before colliding with the huge barrier of Sharrow-Met's arm. There was no time to watch the owl's corpse complete its fall. Stielbek retracted his wings and twisted before going into another dive, streaking down to lash out and snare Rignar's falling body with his talons.

A sound that mixed thunder with the scream of a thousand demons caused Shamil to flatten himself against Steilbek's back, feeling a blast of heat and an intense prickling to the skin. Stielbek banked steeply to the left as another ugly thunderclap sounded, a portion of Sharrow-Met's granite shoulder exploding in a flash Shamil was sure would have blinded him but for his helm's lenses.

Warrior instincts seized him then, all the hard lessons of the Doctrinate and recent experience of battle combining to have him unfurl the whip and deliver a swift backward strike. He saw the topaz tip flare bright as it struck something dark, a silhouette so unexpected in form he barely managed to comprehend the reality of it before it spun away, limbs flailing. He thought it might be one of the man-bats. But, as the shape tumbled in Stielbek's wake, then incredibly, steadied itself and flew in pursuit, Shamil saw no sign of wings. They were being pursued across the sky by a man, a man bearing a staff, the tips blazing white as they poured forth a crackling energy.

The impossibility of the sight caused Shamil to hesitate before lashing out with the whip once more, his confused amazement worsened by the fact that the man was assailing them with words as well as lightning. "Traitor!" he called out as he flew, voice impossibly loud and filled with a depthless rage. "You'll share her fate this day!"

Something in that voice caused Stielbek to rear, spinning about as his wings beat to a blur. Shamil could sense the black wing's fury, a roiling, bitter fire just as deep as that of the flying man. He soared closer as they hovered, staff blazing bright enough to reveal him as the bald-headed mage Shamil recalled so vividly from the day before.

"You think she still lives, traitor?" the Voice-mage asked in a frothing scream, and Shamil saw how his red-glowing eyes were fixed not on him but on Stielbek. "You're a fool! A wretched remnant of her treachery!"

He spun the staff, the tips creating a blazing white wheel Shamil knew instinctively would soon give birth to another lightning bolt.

"She isn't coming to save you!" The bald man's face was every inch as bestial as any Maw beast as he shrieked out his final curse. "Die as she di—"

His words choked off as his rage-filled face formed into a blank, wide-eyed mask of utter astonishment, gaze locked on something in the sky beyond Shamil. Turning, he saw Vintress streaking out of the smoke, Lyvia raised high on her back as she whirled her sling. She had removed her helm, her face revealed in full by the glow of the mage's staff, the face of a woman he insisted was long dead.

He managed to recover his wits just as Lyvia loosed the crystal, raising his staff to deflect the projectile. The staff somehow managed to survive the resultant explosion, as did the mage, but the force of it sent him into a chaotic spin. Lightning coiled and struck in all directions, Shamil's heart lurching as he saw a blazing tendril catch Vintress before she could veer away.

The falcon screeched and spasmed across the sky, disappearing into the shadow cast by the vast statue. Rage burned in Shamil as Stielbek beat his wings and surged forward, closing the distance to the Voice-mage in an instant. He had almost steadied himself now, but not enough to avoid Shamil's whip. It snaked out to coil itself around his staff, the tip blazing out its sorcerous energy as soon as it touched the intricately carved dark wood. Clearly it had already suffered great damage thanks to Lyvia's crystal, for its blazing tips guttered out a final burst of energy before fading. The staff thrummed then shattered, leaving its wielder scrabbling in the air, a wordless scream forming on his lips that choked to a gurgle as the black wing's beak bit deep into his chest.

Stielbek cast the limp doll of the mage's body aside and

soared higher as Shamil looked about desperately for Vintress but could see no sign. His whip trailed in the wind and, seeing the crystal tip destroyed and half of its length burned away, he opened his hand to let it fall. A glimmer of light from beneath Stielbek's bulk caused him to lean forward where he saw Rignar still clutched in the bird's talons. The mage had lost his helm, his gaunt, bleached face staring up at Shamil with imploring eyes. His mouth formed words that were lost to the wind, but the meaning was clear enough as he weakly raised the onyx in his hands.

"Here!" Shamil shouted, crouching and extending his hand to the crystal. "I'll throw it."

Rignar shook his head, the onyx glowing in response as he flattened his hand against its surface. Once again Shamil had no difficulty in reading his unheard words. "I need to be touching it."

"You never intended to throw it!" Shamil shouted back. "Did you?"

Rignar's lips formed a smile as he shook his head.

"Back to the Eyrie!" Shamil shouted at Stielbek. "We'll find another way."

Stielbek angled his wings, but instead of steering for the mountains, he turned back to the statue. "Stop!" Shamil ordered, receiving only an angry shudder in response. "Don't do this!" he cried out to Rignar.

The mage's eyes were sad now, but also shining with a deep contentment, his face that of a man about to fulfil a lifelong task. He removed one hand from the onyx and reached for the chain about his neck, dragging air into his lungs to call out a few words. "The Voice lied, Shamil! She never died!" Rignar snapped the chain and threw it at Shamil. He caught it by pure reflex, finding the emerald pendant dangling in his grip. "She went to find its birthplace!" the mage shouted. "Look for the immortals!"

He stared hard into Shamil's eyes, holding his gaze until the moment Stielbek opened his claws to let him fall free.

Rignar Banlufsson tumbled through the air at a steep angle, the crystal in his hands glowing so bright he resembled a falling star. He collided with the huge, narrow column of granite that formed Sharrow-Met's legendary scimitar barely fifty feet from the point where it met the ground. Crystal and mage disappeared in an explosion powerful enough to banish the smoke for a distance of several hundred yards. Shamil struggled to keep his seat as Stielbek bucked and reared in the turbulent air. Looking down he saw the column of vehlgard closest to the scimitar's base had been blasted into chaotic disorder. The statue, however, remained stubbornly upright.

"It didn't work," he groaned in despair. He scanned the scimitar, finding none of the expectant destruction that would set the great monument toppling. Instead, he saw a curiously smooth and intact surface very different from the weathered granite that had formed it only seconds before. It caught a bright gleam from the sun streaming through the partly dissolved smoke, shining bright, shining like … ice.

"Down!" Shamil ordered, but Stielbek was already folding his wings. A barrage of fire arrows floated up from the ranks of the vehlgard to greet them as they dove, turning to a blizzard as they plummeted lower. Shamil waited until Stielbek levelled out barely fifty feet from the ground before reaching for the sword once carried by Tolveg Clearwater of Wodewehl, a man who had travelled a great distance to place it in more worthy hands, a sword named Ice Cutter in the ancient tongue of his people. A fated blade.

A fire arrow streaked within an inch of Shamil's visor as they swept closer to the scimitar. He hardly noticed, his entire attention focused on the glassy surface, searching. He found the crack near the scimitar's edge, just a small fissure no bigger than a hand's breadth, but big enough for a sword blade. Leaning out, he gripped the sword's handle with both hands, stabbing it into the crack with every ounce of strength he could summon. The *skeln-blad* met scant resistance as it penetrated the ice, sinking so deep it was torn from Shamil's hands as Stielbek beat his wings and bore them higher.

Shamil twisted to watch the scimitar shrink beneath them, his heart leaping in exultant satisfaction at the sight of a web of cracks spreading over its surface. Within seconds the interlocking matrix of fissures had spread from the scimitar's base to its hilt, snaking over it to crumble Sharrow-Met's huge fist.

The statue let out a strange groan as the scimitar fell apart, Sharrow-Met's arm falling to pieces soon after. The great stone queen swayed, rearing back a little and causing Shamil to ponder the horrible irony that she might topple in the wrong direction. But then something cracked deep within her, and she swayed forward, the roar of a huge stone assemblage subsiding into chaos, swallowing the great murmur of surprise and fear rising from the vehlgard army below.

Shamil saw the ice storm fade away then; the Voice-mages rendered scurrying ants at this height as they ran back towards the Maw, but they could never have run fast enough. The statue crushed them beneath its fracturing legs as it collapsed, some of the rubble it shed descending to shatter the columns of vehlgard, but most of its bulk fell where Rignar predicted it would.

The newly wrought bridge of cooled lava disappeared beneath

Sharrow-Met's partly destroyed mass. The rubble settled onto the glowing channel in an ugly dark sprawl that soon began to fade, swallowed by the inexorable tide of molten rock.

Shamil watched the great army of vehlgard convulse as a fresh gout of smoke erupted from the Maw, accompanied by a vast shriek, full of rage and frustration. The vehlgard milled in confusion, some rolling about with their hands clamped to their ears, whilst others thrashed at each other in maddened delirium. Shamil even saw a few march into the lava flow, bursting into flames as the molten rock claimed them but still continuing to wade into the fiery current.

The Voice's scream persisted as Stielbek flew away, the widening distance rendering it a smaller thing, vaguely reminiscent of a spoilt but forlorn child weeping over a broken toy.

The Black Wing's Quest

H E FOUND VINTRESS STRUGGLING BACK TO THE EYRIE
on tired and faltering wings, Lyvia clinging on as the falcon
bobbed in the air. Dark stripes discoloured the verdant
blue of the bird's plumage where the Voice-mage's lightning
had touched her. Still she possessed the strength to keep flying,
although Shamil wasn't sure for how much longer. Steering
Stielbek alongside, he gestured to Lyvia, pointing to the black
wing's claws in an invitation to jump. Lyvia, however, replied
with a stern shake of her head and stayed with her bird.

A dark, fast-moving cloud soon appeared above them, which
had Shamil reaching for his bow and quiver when he realised
it was in fact a dense swarm of flensers and scythers with a few
larger silhouettes that told of man-bats amongst the ugly throng.
He put an arrow to the string of his bow and guided Stielbek

higher to place them between the swarm and Vintress. However, the expected attack never came; the Maw beasts streamed overhead without altering course. Like the vehlgard, they appeared greatly distressed, voicing a cacophony of discordant screams and lashing out at their fellow beasts as they beat their wings towards the Maw. The swarm soon disappeared into the smoke, which now covered the far bank of the lava flow in a thick blanket of soot and ash. The Voice continued to howl its anguish, but the sound had diminished to a plaintive echo by the time Shamil and Lyvia reached the Eyrie.

The sentinels awaited them on the eastward cliff edge, Morgath enclosing Shamil in a tight embrace as soon as he climbed down from Stielbek. He was aware of cheers filling the air and many hands jostling him in appreciation as Morgath guided him through the throng, but it all seemed far away. Exhaustion had risen in him with irresistible force as soon as his boots touched the ground, only fading when he found himself face-to-face with Lyvia.

"Rignar?" she asked, water welling in her eyes when he shook his head.

"He knew," Shamil said, pulling her close to let her sob against him, slender form heaving with a mingling of grief, guilt, and fatigue that mirrored his own. "From the moment we met him, he knew his fate …" He let his voice fade rather than complete the thought aloud, knowing this was not the right time. *As I now know mine.*

◆ ◆ ◆

"YOU WOULD THINK," LYVIA SAID, TURNING THE BRASS disc over to let the moonlight play over the details embossed into its surface, "Ehlias would fashion something more ... fine."

"You disapprove?" Shamil asked. The disc he held was mostly identical to hers, though he noted the smith had taken the time to engrave it with the same runes that had adorned his lost sword.

"No." Lyvia shrugged. "It's just that an object of such importance could benefit from a little more ... artistry."

"Weapons are his art. And I don't think he makes too many of these, especially all at once."

They sat together on the walkway outside the nest. Vintress had secluded herself inside its gloomy confines to nurse her wounds, and Lyvia didn't want to stray too far from her side. Below, the sentinels' celebration continued despite the lateness of the hour. Wine was usually forbidden in the Eyrie, but Morgath had made an exception this night, ordering barrels of impressive vintage be unearthed from the stores and the contents distributed without ration. Raucous hours of merriment followed, interspersed with a surprising amount of brawling as spirits lubricated tongues sufficiently to voice long-nursed grievances. These scuffles were brief if bruising affairs, quickly quelled and soon transformed into weeping expressions of mutual regard. Tihla had taken on the role of policing the gathering, moving amongst the crowd to calm tempers or commiserate over lost comrades. Morgath, by contrast, sat above it all on the highest rise, cup in hand and a bottle at his side. His once ever-cheerful countenance was now a shadowed, brooding mask concealing thoughts Shamil knew must be grim indeed.

"He asked me to return to Mira-Vielle," Lyvia said, noting how Shamil's gaze lingered on the First Wing. "To speak to the council on behalf of the Eyrie, beg for more recruits and a new mage. And to warn them that the Voice has returned. We may have contained it, for now, but only a fool would think it won't try to free itself again."

Hearing the sour weariness in her tone, Shamil said, "You don't want to go."

"Indeed I don't." She brightened a little, twirling the disc in her hand. "And now I have this, I can go where I choose. The north perhaps? See the river of emerald light in the sky Tolveg was always talking about. Or to the south, where a friend of mine tells me the raptorile still roam. Perhaps he would care to guide me?"

Shamil turned away, lowering his head, and the humour had faded from Lyvia's voice when she spoke on. "Except he won't, for I sense he has determined upon another course. No matter." She gave a soft sigh, consigning the disc to her pocket. "I'll do as the First Wing has requested, for I am a sentinel, and when I'm done suffering the company of my noble peers, I shall return here, for this is my home." She glanced back at the opening to the nest. "Besides, Vintress would never leave, and I find I can't be parted from her. As you can't be parted from *him*."

Shamil saw Stielbek shift a little on his perch at the end of the walkway as if hearing the discomfort in Lyvia's tone. As before, he still kept vigil on the Maw but with a restless, constant fidgeting that bespoke a desire to be about more pressing business. His impatience was continually emphasised in the baleful glares he shot Shamil's way throughout the night.

"Rignar said she wasn't dead," he told Lyvia. "Sharrow-Met went to find the Voice's birthplace, presumably to discover a means of destroying it for good. Which begs the question of why she never returned."

"That doesn't mean it's your responsibility to find her."

"No, it's his." He nodded at Stielbek. "That's what he was waiting for all these years, for the Voice to reemerge. He must be far older than anyone here suspected, for this was a task he was set long ago, I suspect by the Wraith Queen herself. The legends say black wings once carried her into battle. It seems she left one behind when she embarked upon her quest."

Stielbek turned a glaring eye upon him then, beak parting to emit a low but commanding hiss. "It appears," Shamil said, stooping to gather up his pack before hefting his bow, "it's time we were on our way."

Lyvia followed him and watched as he climbed onto Stielbek's back, arms crossed as she hugged herself tight. "Where will you look?" she asked.

"Rignar's visions ended when she reached the limit of the eastern desert. As good a place as any to start." Shamil settled his bow on his back before fishing inside his shirt to extract the emerald pendant. It was no bigger than a teardrop and weighed almost nothing, but still he found it sat heavy around his neck. "And I have means of finding more clues if any are needed."

"You will come back." She spoke in soft but emphatic tones that held a demand but no question.

"I will," he promised, putting the pendant away. "And when I do, I expect I'll find you've risen at least to Second Wing."

"That may require me to kill Tihla, and I find I've grown quite fond of her." The laugh rose and died on her lips before she lowered her gaze. "If you do find the Wraith Queen," she said. "Tell her she set an impossible example for her descendants to follow."

"I'll tell her." Shamil glanced at the Eyrie below. The celebration had begun to ebb now, the sentinels staggering off to their chambers, whilst a few lingered to stare in morose contemplation of their fires, some huddling together in shared grief.

"Tell the people of your city the truth," he told Lyvia, turning to the distant glow of the Maw. The Voice's anguished cries had finally subsided along with much of the hateful smoke, only a faint, angry groan issuing from within its depths. Despite this, the absence of Sharrow-Met's statue made the sight of it more foreboding than ever, a signal that their defences had been sorely tested and forever changed.

"Make them hear you." He turned back to Lyvia, staring into her eyes with hard insistence. "You may see the face you wear as a curse, but it needn't be. Bring the Wraith Queen's crusade back to life, for I've a sense it'll be needed again soon."

He may have said more, and so might she, but Stielbek launched himself into the air before any other word could be spoken. He kept his wings folded at first, plummeting down to below the edge of the eastward cliff so no eyes except Lyvia's witnessed their departure. Blinking in the rushing air as Stielbek arced out of the dive, Shamil quickly buckled on his helm. The great bird swept his wings with a slow, regular cadence, flying steadily towards the east. Shamil fought down the urge to look back at the Eyrie in the hope of glimpsing Lyvia's slender form one last time. Instead, he set his gaze on the distant horizon and wondered what he would see when the sun rose to reveal a new landscape come the dawn.

The End

ABOUT THE AUTHOR

Anthony Ryan was born in Scotland in 1970. After a long Career in the UK Civil Service he took up writing full time after the success of his first novel *Blood Song*. His books have been published by Ace/Roc, Orbit, and Subterranean Press. Anthony's work has also been published internationally, being translated into sixteen languages.

For more information on Anthony's books visit his website at: anthonyryan.net.

Follow Anthony on:

Twitter: @writer_anthony

Facebook: www.facebook.com/anthonyryanauthor

Instagram: anthonyryan286

CPSIA information can be obtained
at www.ICGtesting.com
Printed in the USA
LVHW060924230522
719457LV00001B/33